Chapter 1

Beware the Sea

Sophie's face was pressed against the window of an ancient taxi. Her wrists were tied in front of her with a length of old nylon cord. She had spent the last few hours trying to chew through it, when she wasn't shouting at the back of the driver's head. Now it was too late. She knew they were nearly there—wherever *there* was—because the road was running out, petering into rubble until it disappeared into the bloated ocean.

The taxi swerved so fast Sophie hit her head on the window.

"Is this how you're going to kill me?" she shouted at the driver, who she hoped regretted not gagging her. She'd been screaming at him for hours, but everything she said seemed to bounce off his black coat. "I can think of less messy ways to get rid of someone!"

Then she thought of the way he probably *would* get rid of her, by feeding her to one of the ravenous sea creatures that haunted the coast. She started chewing the cord again, trying to pretend that she hadn't already run out of time. As the taxi climbed the hill the sea rose back into view, dark and flat and thick as oil. For a moment Sophie stopped with the rope between her teeth, fascinated by how the water gobbled up the reflection of the moon. She was always getting told off by her parents for staring at the water, but she knew that was because they were terrified of the sea, just like everyone else.

Her eyes refocused and her own face floated into view. There was a deep scratch on her cheek, and her white hair was grimy from being pressed against the seat.

Maybe I've been sold to the circus, she thought, and quickly started chewing again. *Mum always said I looked like a freak.*

She could feel the plastic fibers snapping one by one, but they weren't breaking fast enough. A dull terror reared its head, but she forced it down. If she'd learned anything from school, it was that there was always a way out, whether it was from a locked cupboard or an attack coordinated by the boy whose teeth she knocked out last Sunday. A taxi should be easy.

Through the other window she could see the edge of a grubby seafront town. Most of it was boarded up, but there was a fairground with a roller coaster carriage frozen at the top of a huge drop, and half hidden between houses were bonfires and the occasional electric light. Rubbish was piled up against the buildings, and old bags and scraps of paper tumbled over the gardens. Talismans against the sea creatures were carved into the walls, and huge bags of sand, spilling their guts all over the road, were piled uselessly against the shops and abandoned homes.

As she pressed her teeth into the rope something huge and bright smacked the outside of the window. She jolted with surprise. But it was just a poster flying in the wind.

Don't be stupid, she thought.

She didn't need more than a glance to know what was on that poster. They were everywhere, all across the country, like fungus. That infamous watercolor of an emerald island with blue sky and frothy clouds. Rare butterflies, trees that look suspiciously like lollipops. A twenty-four/seven, blissful holiday paradise.

The poster slid away from the glass, but the picture was still printed across Sophie's inner eyelids: *the New Continent*. The place her parents had gone, abandoning her to start a new life.

The driver slammed the brakes. Sophie's bound hands dropped into her lap. She wriggled into a crouched position, ready to leap up and fight.

"Has anyone told you you're a terrible driver?" she said as he got out the front.

The driver ignored her, inspecting his teeth in the side-view mirror before opening the door and grinning at her. He had the face of someone who knew he was going to enjoy himself.

"I see you've been busy," he said, looking at the chewed cord around her wrists. "Too late. We're here now."

"Is this where you dump every girl you kidnap?"

"Not anymore." The driver leaned in and snapped the cords with his knife. "I'm done with this line of work. I'm off to the New Continent with the fat stash of money your parents gave me."

"You're not," she said. "There aren't any boat tickets left. You'll never get across the sea."

"What would you know? You're just a little girl."

"I'm twelve, actually," she said, raising her chin.

"Ooh," he said mockingly.

Sophie bolted, knocking him over and running toward the town, scrambling through torn-down fences and piles of washed-up oyster shells. The driver shouted and cursed behind her. She swerved, ducked into the shadows, and hid behind a house graffitied with squid ink.

Everything was quiet. Only the sea grumbled to itself over the wind.

She caught her breath and looked around. The town was empty; like her parents, most of the residents had caught Sea Fever and fled. There were shoes abandoned in the middle of the road, and the windows of all the tiny sea-front houses were smashed. Curtains lolled out of the windows like tongues, and there was a terrible stench coming from the boarded-up fishmongers. Now everywhere in the country looked like this, rubbish-strewn and desperate.

Sophie waited for a minute, listening for footsteps, but heard nothing. She turned around slowly, checked the alleyway to either side of her, and slipped around the side of the building.

Right into the arms of the driver.

"Hello," he said, and pointed a gun at her. It stopped her like a brick wall. She thought that looking a bullet in the face would be different. She thought she'd have something clever to say. Instead it felt like her bones had turned to sponge.

They walked down to the beach, the driver just behind Sophie's shoulder, his gun leveled at her head. For the first time in her life she couldn't think of a way to escape, and the realization was suffocating.

"You must be really scared of me if you need a gun," she said. She couldn't help herself. "I'd be embarrassed, if I were you."

"I'll use it if you don't shut up," he snapped.

There was nowhere to run, and nowhere to hide. So she kept going, the cold metal prodding her cheek, on and on as the sea stretched out before them, that huge nightmare that had the world in its thrall. She tried to focus on it.

It's not so bad, really, Sophie told herself, blocking out the gun that wavered on the edge of her vision. *I don't know why everyone wants to escape it so much. It's beautiful.*

But also dark and deadly and ravenous. Sometimes she wondered if her mum was right, that there was something wrong with her to make her so drawn to the sea. It seemed weirdly suitable that she was going to die in the water, anyway.

"Personally, I'd have locked you up to starve somewhere," said the driver, almost conversationally. Sophie realized that he'd been talking for some minutes. "But lucky for you, mummy and daddy have found you somewhere to live while they enjoy their new lives without you. Isn't that nice?"

Sophie was too surprised to say anything.

"Are you deaf?" he asked. "Don't you want to know where you're going?"

To the bottom of the ocean, she thought, *to sleep with the shells and the fish.* She shook herself.

"Where am I going?"

"To the house on Catacomb Hill," he said, and pointed at something in the middle of the sea. Sophie squinted. There was an island, just visible in the gloom, long and dark, sitting in the water like an arched backbone. Perched on its center was a sprawling mansion. The moon above it was a guillotine in the sky, the waves beneath it shivering and black.

"Catacomb Hill," she repeated. Relief flooded through her. He wasn't going to kill her. "Why am I going there?"

"Dunno. Don't care."

But Sophie couldn't—wouldn't—go there. She had to get out of the country, away from the madness and the violence and the shrieking fear of Sea Fever, and she wasn't going to be stopped by some hired thug with a gun. She had to get to the New Continent.

No matter that there were no boat tickets left. She'd deal with that once she got to Portsmouth, where all the ships were.

I'll get there no matter what, she thought. Anger, a constantly bitter lump in her stomach, rose without warning. *I'm going to hunt my parents down and turn up at their new front door and watch my mother faint when she sees me, seaweed in my hair, dripping fish because I've plowed my way through the entire damn ocean to get there!*

She unclenched her fists, which she'd only just realized were hurting. She tried to smile sweetly, but her mouth wasn't used to the shape.

"You've done your job," she told the driver. "You took me away from my home and dumped me Neptune-knows-where. Why can't you just leave me on the beach? It'll be easier for both of us."

"'Cause I'm not an idiot." The driver gestured at the house on the island. "You'll go running back to your parents, that's what you'll do, and they'll know I didn't finish the job. You've been sold, and I'm making sure you reach the buyer." They stopped walking. The air seemed like it was holding its breath. "There's a path through the water that will be clear for, oh . . ." he checked his watch. "Another ten minutes? So you'd better get going."

Sophie turned to look at the water. If she concentrated she could just about make out a slick of rock running from the beach into the sea. It was a tidal path, the kind that gets swallowed by the water when the sea rises, so you can never turn back.

"Start walking," said the driver.

"Make me," she said automatically.

The driver sighed and prodded her in the back with his gun. Sophie turned to face him, still thinking she might be able to reason with him, but he looked impatient and she suddenly doubted her powers of persuasion. She took a step backward. And another. They edged toward the sea until the water was lapping at her heels.

"You'll like it on Catacomb Hill," the driver said. "Interesting place. There's a whole family living there. The old man killed himself, and they go through servants like they're putting 'em through a sausage machine. That's right. You're not the first. They have a bit of a monster problem, so I reckon they'll feed you to the sea. There's rumors, you know, about the people on that island. That they're all mad."

He cocked the gun. Sophie turned and walked into the sea as calmly as she could. The narrow path into the ocean was very thin, and very slippery, and in all probability led to nowhere but death.

She swallowed and turned to the beach one last time.

"I forgot to tell you," she said. "After you so kindly

pressed my face against the floor of your car this morning, I looked under the seat and found the money my parents gave you. You might have tied my hands up, but you forgot about my teeth."

She spat out a shred of green-and-white paper, and had just enough time to see the driver's mouth open with fury before she ran into the sea, his gunshots hitting the water behind her.

Chapter 2

Welcome to Catacomb Hill

Sophie cautiously walked along the wet line of rock that split the sea. She knew there were dark and dreadful things below her, whale-sized fish and whirlpools, plants with mouths, and sea snails as huge and old as the rocks themselves. All she had to do was get to the house on the island, but dread had made her freeze up.

Move, she willed herself, but now that she was halfway across her knees wouldn't even bend. *I'm being stupid. There's nothing to be scared of.*

Except there was. Even if she got to the island without being eaten, she'd be trapped until the path came back. She'd never catch up with her parents, and the last boats would leave without her. She wasn't even comforted by imagining their fear as they crossed the sea. *I bet they're stuffing their faces on the New Continent right now. The pigs!*

She looked at the shore. The driver and his taxi were gone, but so was the path. It was closing behind her like a zipper. Her ribs crumpled in on her when she realized there was no way but forward.

She forced herself to move toward the island. The path was coated in fresh seaweed, and every time she put a foot down she slipped. The stench of kelp mixed with rotting fish was so overwhelming she had to breathe through her hand. She recalled tales of sea draugrs, undead sailors that preyed on children out after dark, and quickened her pace.

The sea was no longer calm, but rose and fell like it was excited to have someone to play with. Water lapped at her feet. Sophie fixed her eyes on the house on the island, trying to ignore the vastness of the sea on either side of her. *If there's anything here*, she told herself, *it'll be sleeping at the bottom of the ocean with its tail curled around its nose, dead to the world. Not worrying about me.*

Left foot, right foot, slip, slide. The house was slowly growing in detail. It was monstrously big, haunted-looking, and decayed to the point of ruin. There was one light burning on the top floor. Left foot. Right foot. She was making better progress now, and she felt, just for a second, more confident.

Something caught her eye, and she dodged as a dark

shape whipped over her head. Black tentacles rose from the churning sea and slithered toward her, slapping the ground at her feet. *Monsters!* Sophie stumbled back, tripped, and fell into the water. The water was so cold it felt like being stabbed. She scrambled up, her ankles already stiff, her lungs like blocks of ice.

But she wouldn't let them get her—not without a fight. She clenched her teeth and raised her fists as she plowed forward, ignoring the freezing water around her knees.

A tentacle lashed itself around her ankle. She screamed and wrenched it free, and heard a roar like a cliff falling away from the earth. She ran, but a wave came after her, and the sea hit her with deafening force. She was thrown from the path and tossed in the brine.

The whole world turned upside down. For a moment her eyes were still open, and she could see a chaos of junk—an old suitcase thrown open, a strand of beads, a doll's face attached to a limp body. She struggled to kick to the surface in her wet clothes. It was too far away. She was about to take a lungful of water, the first step toward drowning.

And then, as fast as it came, the sea dropped away and left her strewn on the side of the path like a piece of rubbish.

Sophie hauled herself up and ran toward the house. It

grinned like an old man with no teeth. The ocean crowded around it, drumming against the island as though trying to smash it to pieces. She plunged into a pool that had started to run over the vanishing path. It was deeper than she'd expected, and she had to swim. Her foot caught on something with hooks, and as the water swelled again she wrenched her boot off and threw herself forward with only one shoe on. The next wave just missed her.

And now she was on her feet again, the path illuminated by a cold and metallic moon, bits of broken shell cutting her, the wind lifting the water from her skin and making her body sting. Her fingers were frozen, clothes dragging her down, eyes nearly blinded by salt, and on top of all *that*, someone had extinguished the light on the island so she didn't know where to run to.

If I get out of this, if I ever see my parents again, they won't have time to scream before I throw them into the water!

But she knew nobody would pay for what they'd done. The thought made her clench her fists.

The path had degenerated into a patch of sharp points. The driver had lied to her. The only way to escape was to drown.

She turned to face the distant beach she'd run from. The sea slapped against her feet in merriment. Her other boot, which had come unlaced, was sucked off her foot and bobbed away. In a matter of minutes she'd be under.

"Come on, then!" she screamed, raising her arms. Her voice bounced between the waves and returned amplified. "Come and get me, you pathetic creatures!"

The water hit her in the knees. She gritted her teeth, which were chipped from her last fight.

Then something cold hit the back of her neck, and she was wrenched from the water.

Sophie opened her eyes to a sky like spilled ink. She could have been asleep for an eternity.

Her head hurt. Her arms and legs hurt. All she knew was that she should be angry or scared about something, but she couldn't remember what. She lifted her head to check that the rest of her body was there. She was wearing an ugly old dress, the one her parents always made her wear. She'd made them upset for some reason. What did she do?

She scraped through her memories. She was a storyteller. She lived in London. No, she used to, but it wasn't her home anymore. Why was that?

I got in the way of something.

She remembered her mum calling her sarcastic and stupid. A freak, full of useless stories. A girl who hated dresses and liked wearing boys' clothes and causing trouble. She didn't mean to be any of these things, but she was.

She rolled over and groaned.

Maybe it was the way she looked. People used to sneak up on her in school, before everyone left and it closed down, and cut chunks of her long, snow-white hair off with scissors. After the third time she told everyone her hair was cursed, and they stayed clear of her.

It could have been worse. They could have known about her extra toes.

There was something else.

Her parents had caught Sea Fever—the terrible epidemic that made everyone afraid of the water. Her pet fish had been thrown away. Even cups of tea became objects of terror. Her parents, in the grip of the fever, sold her off to buy boat tickets for the New Continent.

She remembered the taxi driver, and the fog in her head began to clear.

They got angry and forced me into his car. And after that—

The sea, the moon like a guillotine in the sky. A gun and a bad-tempered squid.

That's right.

She looked around. She was on Catacomb Hill, which

rose steeply from the waves, and there was a dark, ugly building behind her. The memories struck her like a brick, and she rolled over to vomit weakly into the grass. From here, her cheek pressed to the ground, she could see everything.

The house was made of wet, black stone, and where there should have been gargoyles there were stone fish and tentacled monsters leering at the sea. It was at least five floors tall and unimaginably wide. The whole building looked like it was about to slip into the water, with leaning walls and great holes in the roof that had vegetation poking out the top. Everything was made furry by a layer of moss, and there was a pervasive smell of damp and mold. It looked like a house lost in the jungle. It was terrifyingly grand and wild.

The island itself was curved like a boomerang, stretching out on either side of her, a forest of overgrown scrubland. She was in an unkempt garden at the front of the house, where the plants were black and crispy as though they'd been burned. Everything in front of it sloped into the sea.

Sophie raised herself to her knees, then ducked her head when she saw something move below. There was a clicking sound like a rusty wheelbarrow being pushed through the garden, and a low muttering like a radio nobody was listening to.

"Only people going to cross the sea tonight is dead people. The sea's mean and it'll come after 'em like one of 'em beady magpies. Thought they'd bring someone over? Thought they'd buy another servant for me?"

The voice barked laughter, coughed, laughed again. Sophie crawled to the edge of the bank, dragging herself through purple thistles, and peered over. Below her was an elderly man, his legs long and spindly like a spider's, his head as bare as a rock. He was fishing in the sea with a monstrous grab-claw contraption on a pole. The claw snapped at things in the water while the old man struggled to hold it up.

"They've sent another body to be fished out of the water by poor Mister Scree, that's what they've sent, and he has to bow and scrape and pretend everything's wonderful— 'oh yesh, Your Battleshipness, don't worry, Scree *loves* fishing for the dead.'" Another coughing fit ensued. "Idiots."

The man—all sticks and papery skin, crunching when he moved as though he was preserved by salt—jabbed the claw at something in the water and dragged out a saucepan. He stopped just above the waterline and peered at the mainland, the smokestacks and factories, the boarded-up shops.

"Pretty lights," he cooed. Then he checked his barnacle-crusted pocket watch. "It's feeding time soon, oh yes, pretty fishies. I haven't forgotten you." He took a cloth from his pocket and began to polish the pointed stones that almost ripped Sophie to pieces.

Sophie crawled backward. This man was clearly as mad as a box of frogs. She glanced at the house, but the door looked impenetrable.

"She's woken up," said the old man. Startled, Sophie turned back and found that he was looking right at her. "Welcome to Catacomb Hill. I was about to throw you back as fish food."

Unsure what to do, she climbed down the bank and fell over the pile of rubbish the man had collected at the bottom. She landed by his shoes, which were splitting and held together with string.

"Am I dead?" she asked, scrambling up with her foot inside a copper kettle.

"I wouldn't know about stuff like that," he said, dragging the claw through the water.

"Did you pull me out?"

He stopped to evaluate her, from her bruised legs to her white hair. She jutted her chin out and glared.

"I might have," he said finally. "Not that I'll get thanks for it. You here to be useful, then?"

"I don't know why I'm here. I was kidnapped and dragged here at gunpoint—" she broke off to cough up more water. She felt like she'd been run over by a truck.

"Where're your shoes?"

She looked at her feet.

"The sea got them."

He chewed his tongue for a moment.

"Yep, it'll do that. Never heard no one talk to the creachers before, though. You'd better be nice to 'em, now you've charged past 'em without asking."

Sophie stared at him. She tried to replay the conversation and got lost. Nobody apart from her had ever spoken about the sea as though it could hear them.

"What's your name?" she asked finally.

"Her Battleship calls me the General."

"You're in the military?"

"No, she calls me that 'cause I'm so general," he said. "Dogsbody, cleaner, feeder of fish—I'm not posh enough for *military*. My name's Scree."

"I'm Sophie Seacove—"

"Ha!" he barked, for no apparent reason.

"—and I need to get off this island!"

"You'll have to wait. Tide's swallowed the path, and it only comes around every six months. There's only one person can cross the sea now, and I bet all the fish in the big blue wet thing that he won't be of any use!"

Sophie's legs gave way and she sat down with a thump.

"I don't believe you," she said angrily. "There must be a way back."

"The path ain't coming back any time soon," he repeated. "No sailing 'cause our boat's been chewed up. Can't swim, either. Too dangerous." He leaned on the claw pole like it was a walking stick, while it snapped away at his foot. "I'll tell you what you're here for. The Battleship bought you to help me with my duties. I'nt that nice?"

"What duties?"

"Mealtimes."

"Is that a joke where it turns out I'm the meal?"

But Scree had gone, trundling up the garden path, his knees making that rusty wheelbarrow sound.

"Hey!" Sophie called. "Does that mean I . . . hello?"

She ran after Scree, scrambling up the bank, pushing through overgrown thistles and tripping over weeds. The rubble turned into cobblestone, and then into steps. Out of the darkness loomed stone busts with smooth eyes and waterfalls of black ivy for hair. Strewn over the ground were bones—real-life, bigger-than-big bones. One of them rolled under her foot.

"It's okay," she said to herself, a bit too loud. "This is *completely fine and normal.*"

Scree stopped at the door. His eyes were glowing like wet fish.

"Are you coming in?" he asked. "I wouldn't wait too long to make your mind up. They'll get hungry and come looking for you."

"The sea creatures?"

There was a screech from the sea, and it bounced around the curve of the island. Scree's eyes flicked toward the horizon, and Sophie realized that he was nervous.

"I only want to know how to get out of here," she insisted.

"I'm not talking to you until we're inside. They're getting antsy, and I want to keep my legs."

He drew a huge bunch of keys from his pocket. They were so heavy they made him double up. He sorted through them until he found the right one, then wriggled it into the keyhole, twisting the key with both hands. There was a deep grinding sound, and the door shivered for a moment before opening. Behind it there was nothing, only a deep and colorless void.

"I'm not meant to be here," Sophie said, imagining the boats sailing to the New Continent without her. She ached to reach out and slam the door, to turn back and run into the sea.

"But here you are," said Scree. He tapped his foot as he held the door open. Sophie looked over her shoulder at the sea and the distant, dilapidated town. There was a low rumbling sound, and the water started to foam.

"I'm coming," Sophie said.

She climbed the steps and the darkness reared up to greet her. Scree pulled her through by the shoulder before she could change her mind and slammed the door. They were standing in sudden, perfect stillness, the air heavy like a damp blanket. Already she felt the cloying need to wring her lungs out.

"From now on, if you like your skin, you don't go outside 'cept to do your job," said the voice of Scree. Sophie raised her hands but there was nothing to hold on to, only the feeling of space. "You don't even look through the keyhole, 'cause the sea creatures watch the hole like hawks. 'Cept they're cleverer than hawks. Are you ready to meet the house?"

Sophie wasn't ready. Escape plans were knotting themselves together in her head, but she couldn't sort them out.

It felt like her tongue had turned to dust in her mouth.

"Stop gawping," Scree said. "I've got a tour planned and everything."

"And then we'll talk?"

"If you want," he said. "But I don't see what good it'll do."

There wasn't one part of him that she trusted, but she didn't have a choice. Part of her was glad that she didn't have to face the night again.

"I'm ready," she said.

Scree put a match to a lantern, and so began the grand tour.

Chapter 3

The Grand Tour

The house on Catacomb Hill was as quiet as the bottom of the sea. Sophie was stranded in a circle of yellow light, her crooked shadow flickering uncertainly. Scree finished locking the door, which was crossed with pulleys and levers, and took the lantern from her cold fingers.

"Your new home," he said as the light sputtered and crept into the corners of the room. "It's a bit damp, but you'll get used to it."

They were standing in a cavernous entrance hall the length of Sophie's entire home. The ceiling was so far away she couldn't see it, and the walls were covered in peeling green wallpaper that made the house look ill. The carpet was also green, and wet, and something—it felt like a crab—crawled over her feet. There were suits of armor lined up against the walls, slumped like they'd been shot in the back. She tried to calculate the weight of their swords and wondered if she could swing one hard enough to decapitate a sea creature.

"Well?" said Scree.

Well what? It looked to Sophie like a place forgotten by the rest of the world. The kind of place where people went moldy if they stood still for too long.

"It's big," she said.

"It's not for you. You're living in the catacombs with me."

In the middle of the grand hall was a splayed-out staircase with black banisters sprouting wrought-iron tentacles and decorative oyster shells. Something stirred in Sophie's memory, and then it was gone. Still, she had the lingering feeling that she knew this place, as if she'd seen a photo of a photo of a photo. The walls shivered, ever so slightly, like she was standing in the body of a great and dangerous beast.

She went to touch the banisters, but Scree huffed and she stopped.

"What's wrong?"

"You're making the carpet wet," he said.

The floor was shining with water as far as the end of the room. A fleet of tiny, bronze-colored fish skidded across the floor and vanished into a hole in the wall, through which another gray staircase disappeared, this time into the ground. A brass plaque with a green beard read: *The Catacombs. By appointment only.*

She tore her gaze away and found Scree watching her craftily, like he'd figured something out.

"What?" she said again, more perturbed than she wanted to be.

"You can feel it, can't you," he said. "The house."

The walls shivered again. Yes, she could feel something, but she couldn't put her finger on it. If she had to describe it, she would say that it breathed in time with the wash of the sea. But that was stupid. It was a *house*.

"I sort of—"

Scree twitched and raised a finger. Sophie froze, and he jerked his head toward the entrance of the catacombs with his lips curling upward.

"The bones are getting restless," he said. "They clatter around when they think I'm not listening, but Scree knows they're there. Think if they sing and dance I won't throw them to the monsters."

"I can't hear anything," she said.

"You must have barnacles in your ears," he said. "Don't move until I come back. I know what you're like. I can see the trickiness in your eyes."

He closed his calloused fist over the flame in the lantern, which went out and left the smell of burning paper. Suddenly blind, Sophie reached out again to grab onto something, but she was alone in the middle of the room.

"Mister Scree?" she hissed.

She took a step forward, and the wet carpet squished up between her toes. As her eyes adjusted, she began to see damp, flabby curtains with mold growing on them, and behind them, through the cracked and dirt-covered window, the white moon under a cloud.

How long would the batty old man be gone for? Her eyes slid to the stairs that reached up and into the heart of the house. She'd never been any good at keeping still, and her feet were itching to move.

She crossed to the stairs, trailing her hand over the lumpy banister, and began to climb. The spongy carpet announced her presence with a series of rude squelches. It occurred to her that the old man could be alone in the house, and "Her Battleshipness," whoever she might be, was his imaginary friend. What then? What if Scree wasn't just mad but totally, unspeakably insane?

A hoot of laughter seesawed down the stairs, cut short by breaking glass. Sophie stopped with her foot in the air, and the noise happened again, this time with shouting.

Two voices, identically high-pitched, howled curses at each other. The next crash dislodged a lump of plaster from far above.

Sophie climbed swiftly to the top of the first flight and crouched behind the banister. The hall stretching off to her right was an unlit tunnel, but to her left it was lined with fat yellow candles, a Hansel-and-Gretel-style trail that stopped at a door. She knew that it would be stupid to creep up to the door, and even worse to press herself against the wall to listen. So that's what she did, bending low as the candles danced beside her.

Crash!

"Three points!" someone shrieked, and there was a high giggle that rose and fell like a yo-yo.

"Bonus five if you get it in the eye!" the second voice said, and there was more laughter, a *thwack*, the sound of shattering glass.

"Gail, that's her vase, you idiot. It's priceless!"

"Ten extra points!" screamed Gail.

That nasal laugh again. It was so high-pitched it made Sophie's jaw ache.

Crash!

"Your aim is rubbish, Gail."

Thwack!

There was a pained scream.

"Good thing your head's such a huge target, Ralf!" said Gail.

"You little—"

Something dropped in front of Sophie's face and crawled over her lips. She spluttered and inhaled a furry spider, then coughed and clawed it out of her mouth. It fell and ran across the floor, but even so she could still feel it in there, its legs dancing on her tongue. When she'd finished raking her tongue across her sleeve, a new feeling settled on the corridor. It was the feeling of being listened to.

After a long pause the door containing the voices swung open very slowly. Nobody came out. It was an invitation. They were waiting for Sophie to show herself. She looked over her shoulder, suspecting some kind of trick. Seeing nothing but empty gloom, she walked through the doorway.

The room was a lot brighter than she'd expected, and for a moment she was dazzled. Then, as her vision cleared, she saw the twins.

Tall and skinny, they were dressed in faded red suits that must have come from the bottom of a costume box, their sleeves stopping a couple of inches above their wrists and their too-short trousers exposing green socks. Their hair was red and so messy it looked like they'd recently escaped a storm. They were exactly alike, except one had *R* embroidered on his lapel, and the other *G. Ralf and Gail.* Gail stood somewhat slumped. His eyes flicked toward his brother, who was twirling a tennis racket between his fingers.

Ralf grinned at Sophie, his mouth snapping open in a smile that showed all his teeth at once.

"It looks like mother's found us another toy to play with," he said.

"What is it? Is it a girl, Ralf?" asked Gail. His fingers wriggled like worms on a hook.

"Yes, I think so. Doesn't it have weird hair? I've never seen hair like *that* before."

"You're right. Why does it have white hair?"

The twins looked at her expectantly. Sophie realized that they were even breathing at the same time, exhaling together like clockwork. They were waiting for an answer.

"I saw a ghost," she said as a piece of squashed fruit dropped from the ceiling. It landed in the wreckage with a terminal plop.

The room must have been beautiful once, but now it was a total mess: there was a smashed chandelier, scorch marks in the carpet, dents in the walls, and a painting of a rather pained-looking horse with a rolled-up napkin wedged onto its forehead, where it had apparently been smashed with a tennis racket. In the corner of the room a brass machine spat another napkin out, where it hit the wall with a sad and unnoticed *thump*.

The twins smelled like formaldehyde, the chemical Sophie's dad used to preserve his award-winning carrier pigeon with when it died.

"I have to find Mister Scree," she said, suddenly feeling uneasy. "He's waiting for me."

Ralf reached out and grabbed her arm. His nails were sharp and left little crescents in her skin. Sophie flushed with anger, but she forced herself to keep still.

"Never mind Scree," Ralf said. "He's just an old coffin-dodger who thinks he runs the place. You can help us. We're rehearsing a play."

"A play?"

"A play?" mimicked Ralf, his face twisting into a shape that, for a moment, Sophie recognized perfectly as her own reflection. It was so good she caught her breath. Then, in a second, it had gone.

"We're going to be famous actors," said Gail. "We'll go to London and take the country by storm. Won't we, Ralf?"

"We will," Ralf said. "There'll be posters of us on every street. We'll rule the world."

"When our play's good enough, that is."

Sophie tried to take Ralf by surprise by wrenching her arm away suddenly, but his grip was too tight.

"We've been practicing for years," he continued.

"But not because we're no good," said Gail.

"We're just not *ready*."

"But when we are—"

"—we'll be unstoppable."

They both gave her frozen smiles, and Ralf's nails dug a little deeper.

"You should let go of me before I get annoyed," Sophie growled, although there was clearly no way out.

"What we need," Ralf said, ignoring her, "is someone to do a drowning with. There's a girl called Ophelia in our play, and she throws herself into a river. It's our favorite bit."

"We wrote it ourselves," said Gail. "It's a great play."

"Yes, but we can't act that part, can we? We need a girl to run around and scream."

Without warning, Ralf released her. Sophie dodged away, clutching her wrist.

"Where's she going, Ralf?"

"I don't know, Gail. She's being awfully rude, isn't she?"

"Maybe we ought to teach her a lesson."

"Maybe we ought to flush her head down the toilet like we did with our cousin."

"Cartwright? Oh, that was fun. He should be here again soon."

"She'll love Cartwright, won't she, Gail. All the servants do."

"But I hope she's not *too* much like the others. We can't have her running off and ruining our play."

"I can't think of anything that would make me more annoyed."

The twins gave her a look that was truly murderous.

Sophie stepped backward out of the room, then tripped on a broken chair leg and fell right into Scree. Ralf and Gail spluttered with laughter.

"Found the skeletons rattling around in the catacombs," Scree said proudly, swooping so close Sophie couldn't see anything except his eyes. "Caught 'em all. Nothing can run without a rib cage!" He picked up the sack at his feet and gave it a cheerful shake.

"Scree!" Ralf yelled from inside. "We want toast and pineapples for tea!"

"Pineapples, sir?"

"They're yellow and they come from trees. You idiot."

The twins started smashing the room again, swinging

their tennis rackets at the napkins flying out of the machine.

"Interesting, aren't they?" Scree said.

Sophie whirled around and backed Scree against the wall until they were nose-to-nose.

"No," she said. "They're creepy. And that's a nice way of putting it."

"They won't like you saying that."

"I don't care. You said you'd talk to me, so talk. Tell me how to get away from this place and I'll do it, even if I have to swim."

She realized that she was facing a blank wall. Scree had slid away like a bar of soap, and she was just in time to see him scurry down the unlit side of the hallway. She took off after him, hiking her skirt up above her knees.

Scree stopped around the corner so suddenly she almost ran into him.

"Here's a nugget of advice," he said. "When you're with the twins, pretend you're stupid. They're thirteen now, and they've grown a fine temper. Neptune help you if you upset 'em."

"I'm not going to pretend anything," Sophie said. "Where are you going?"

"I'm going to show you something," he said, jabbing his thin finger into her chest. "Just to wipe any nonsense about escaping out of your head. Are you brave enough?"

"I've never been scared of anything," she said.

Scree's eyes burned through her. She stared right back, and finally he looked away.

"Make sure you keep up," he muttered.

And they began moving again, deeper and deeper into the house on Catacomb Hill.

The screeching of the twins died away as they wormed into the moonlit labyrinth of the house. Scree moved quickly, ducking and diving through curtains of cobwebs, with Sophie following behind. The green carpet slowly became blue, and she realized that it was just no longer covered in algae. They went past dozens of locked rooms—Sophie knew, because she tried each doorknob—and into a corridor lined with portraits. Each face was pocked with spots of mold or growing a furry mustache. She recognized the twins when they were younger, both thin as rakes, their cheekbones straight like carving knives. Between them was an older man who was remarkably dissimilar to them: brown hair, round glasses, a nervous smile.

"Does he live here, too?" Sophie asked.

Scree grunted and carried on.

The house grew and grew before her eyes, each corridor sprouting stuffed fish, shells in picture frames, and furniture made from worryingly human-looking bones.

"Where do all the bones come from?" she asked.

"From the catacombs under the island. Before this house was built on top, they were a place to leave the dead." Scree cackled. "His lordship Laurel wanted somewhere grand to live."

He shook the sack of bones again.

"So a man called Laurel built this ugly mansion," she said. "He built it on an island full of holes, filled with dead bodies, in a lethal creature-infested sea. Am I missing anything?"

"He was a genius," said Scree. "An inventor. He was famous once. He filled this place with machines and plumbing and clockwork, though it mostly doesn't work now. And he left old Scree a gift to help him do his job."

"Is the floor shaking?"

"Eh? Course it is."

They stopped outside a particularly large door. From inside came the sound of ticking and the grinding of machinery. Sophie, with a nod from Scree, put her eye to the keyhole.

When her eyes adjusted, she realized she was looking at the inside of a vast and complicated clock. Pulleys and levers stretched from floor to ceiling, and there were spinning cogs and weights bobbing up and down next to a corroded bell the size of a wardrobe. The floor plunged into a bottomless hole, with a walkway swinging precariously above it. Hourglasses danced on strings, and one flipped over neatly to reverse the flow of sand.

"I *knew* the house was moving," she said triumphantly. She tried the door handle, but it was locked. "What's this for?"

A weight turned over. The shaking grew until it made her teeth chatter.

"I'd cover my ears if I were you," said Scree.

The bell inside the clockwork room rang.

It started as a vibration going up her knees and into her stomach. She stuffed her fingers into her ears just in time, because a second later a deafening wave of sound threw her to the ground. She clenched her teeth as her whole body vibrated with the shifting floorboards.

The noise died away, but it felt like her head was stuffed with cotton wool. She looked up and could see Scree talking, but heard nothing until he clapped her around the head with his bony hand.

"I *said*, get up and follow me. That bell's the five-minute warning; that's what your new job sounds like. The Bone Snatching."

She could tell he'd given this talk before. He seemed to be enjoying himself.

"The what?" she shouted back.

"No need to shout," he said. "Come on, we haven't got all night. The monsters are very exacting when it comes to dinnertime."

Sophie wobbled after Scree as fast as she could. They twisted and turned and came to a damp room overhanging the sea.

"I don't want anything to do with bones," said Sophie, but Scree wasn't listening. He undid latch after latch on an enormous window, so many of them that it seemed like they'd been designed to keep something out.

"Normally we do this close up on the beach," he said. "The monsters like the personal touch. But tonight I'm treating you to a good view."

"Of what?" she said.

"You got any experience in the culinary industry?"

"No. Only in storytelling."

"Storytelling," he repeated. His fingers paused on the window frame, and Sophie was taken aback by the sadness in his expression. "I ain't heard a story in a while.

His lordship liked stories." He trailed off, gazing into the sea below. Then irritation puckered his face again. "What kind of stories?"

"All kinds," said Sophie, papering over her surprise. "I'm going to be a storyteller on the New Continent. I'm going to record history, so that nobody forgets what it was like before Sea Fever struck."

"A historian," Scree said.

"Yeah, that sounds good. A historian of sanity."

Scree shrugged, telling her the conversation was over, then jammed his hands under the glass window and pulled with his whole body.

The frame shot upward, and a blast of cold air hit them. He picked up the sack and heaved it onto the windowsill, turning back to make sure he had Sophie's full attention. Then he upended the sack and a pile of bones— gray and yellow, cracked and broken—tumbled to the ground and bounced to the rocks by the shore.

The sack slipped from his fingers and drifted into space. Scree slammed the window shut, as though he wanted to get as far away from the sea as possible.

He stood back to let Sophie watch.

The sea churned and pulsed, growing blacker. A shadow, huge as a submarine, writhed under the water. It spread and became a creature: There was a spine, and there were spikes, black and oily, that punctuated the surface with bursts of foam and scum. Long tapered legs uncurled from its sides, dragging clumps of seaweed and debris in its wake.

Sophie recoiled, but Scree planted a hand on her shoulder.

"It ain't done yet."

The size of a normal house, now, the thing broke the surface, bobbing like an ice floe, its body constantly changing shape. Water poured from its back as its eyes rolled wildly. One dark orb settled on Sophie, and it heaved itself from the water with a supernatural groan that shook the walls.

It moved so fast she couldn't make out its shape. Tentacles shot toward the rocks. The scattered bones were dragged toward the sea with chunks of stone and torn-up bushes. One after the other, more things rose from the water, some the size of horses, others as small as her hand, all armed with tentacles, squid-like and bristling with barnacles. They were fighting to get to the food first. The biggest creature's body plummeted back into the depths, legs slapping the water like pieces of elastic, gripping the scraps. And then it was gone, the water foaming and the rest of the monsters fighting in its wake, crabs surging over the remains like rats over bread.

"We had boats once," Scree said. "They tore them up years ago. But it don't matter, 'cause there's nothing on the mainland for the likes of you and me but misery. No New Continent for us, 'cause we ain't important enough. But here we have a job. We feed 'em best we can to stop 'em tearing down the house, and when we run out of food, which ain't too far away to be honest, the monsters'll swim to the front door." He paused, then added bitterly, "We'll be sucked out of our beds and that's that."

"That's not true," Sophie said fiercely. "You said there's someone who knows how to get across the sea."

"He only comes here to stir up trouble," he said. "Trust me. It won't end well."

"I'm going to escape," she said, gripping the windowsill as flecks of water flew up from the sea.

"All the servants say that," Scree said. "You think whatever you want to. We all tell ourselves stories here."

Chapter 4

The Rules of the House

Sophie was a Bone Snatcher, a feeder of monsters.

Her home was in a cave far beneath the house on Catacomb Hill. The house itself was only the tip of the island; the rest plunged far beneath the water like the roots of an old tooth. Tunnels folded back against themselves like intestines, nightmare dark and endless, crammed together in a space that shouldn't be able to contain all that distance.

Sophie's room was carved straight into the rock. Her bed was a slab worn smooth by hundreds of sleepers. She lay there for what remained of the first night, staring at the ceiling as waves lapped against the other side of the wall.

She wouldn't be in this creepy place if Sea Fever hadn't struck. Before then, people had tolerated the sea creatures;

now everyone was so mad with terror they wouldn't even turn the taps on.

By now her parents would be boarding one of the last ships to the New Continent, clutching the tickets they'd sold her off for. Her mum and dad flickered behind her eyelids like holograms, pulling their trunks behind them as they entered Portsmouth. In a few hours the land would have disappeared from view. They would sail on while terror squeezed their hearts dry, until the great, monster-free shores of the New Continent rose from the sea.

The thought of her parents' ship in the endless, gray sea made her hands cold and her eyes blurry.

At some point she must have fallen asleep, because when she next opened her eyes there was light creeping in from upstairs. Sophie sat up quickly, banging her head on the rock and yelping.

Scree, hidden behind the doorway, banged his fishing claw against the floor.

"Uh?" she said, trying desperately to remember where she was.

"You're late," he said grumpily. "I've got to train you."

"Train me for what?" she said.

"Do you pay attention to anything?" He shook his head and came hobbling over. "You don't just chuck rubbish in the water. You've got to know what the sea creatures want that day. On calm days they like nice long bones and bobbing skulls. When the storms come they want armor and sharp things. You treat 'em well, show 'em respect, and they'll do the same for you, s'long as you don't push your luck. And you've gotta know when feeding time is near. Five minutes after the bell rings, that's all the time you've got, or they'll get annoyed and start looking for chunks of the house to munch on instead."

"What do they have as stomachs? Cement mixers?"

"Could well be," he said humorlessly. "They eat anything. They've taken three pairs of false teeth from me. I saw an octopus wearing 'em the other day, smirking like a cat in a sardine factory."

With that he disappeared, and Sophie fell out of bed while trying to untangle herself from her old, damp clothes. There was a crate in the corner overflowing with bits of tattered material. She pulled them out: dozens of old outfits belonging to people of every shape and size, a litany of the things left behind by other visitors to Catacomb Hill. There were no trousers that fit her, so she tore the lace off a yellowing, salt-crusted dress and put it on with a camel hair coat. The only shoes she could find pinched and had a hole in the toe.

She followed Scree's wet footprints out of the catacombs

49

and emerged in the house, where he was waiting with a bowl of porridge so thick the spoon was standing upright. Her stomach growled, but when she reached out for it he lifted it over his head.

"There's three rules in this house," he said. "One: Don't go knocking on closed doors."

"Right," she said, knowing that she wasn't going to follow any of his rules.

"Two: Don't talk to anyone. Not the twins, 'cause they'll play you like a fiddle, and not the Battleship, 'cause she'll pull your head off and use it as a doorstop. Got it?"

"Uh-huh," she said.

"Are you actually listening?"

"Yes!"

"Three: Don't be late for the Bone Snatching. I'll feed the monsters breakfast today, but you can help me with their lunch, and after that you're on your own. I'll be waitin' on the oyster beach for you. As soon as the bell rings, leg it down here. Understand?"

Sophie nodded, and he grudgingly gave her the gray porridge. It looked like there were a couple of fish bones in it. Her stomach screwed itself up, and she had to turn her head so she couldn't smell it. Maybe she could go a bit longer without food.

50

"What happens if I'm late?" she said.

"I'll unscrew your ears and use 'em as fish bait," he said. "Any questions?"

"Yes. When I'm not feeding the monsters, what am I supposed to *do*?"

"None of my business," Scree said. "All I do is fish 'n' make the dinner. You just sit in a corner somewhere until you're needed."

"A corner," Sophie said. "Brilliant."

"You don't want to go pokin' around. You'll regret it. This place is full of deep 'n' terrible secrets."

"Mister Scree, that's enough to make anyone want to go poking around."

"Ain't none of my business," he repeated, and stalked away with an unreadable scowl.

There was a courtyard in the middle of the house, shaded and dank with trapped rainwater. Sophie ended up there like a marble rolling toward the center of a bowl. No matter where she turned she was facing the courtyard again, looking at the paved square through a hundred different windows. It was like the house was always shrugging, tipping her where it wanted her to go. Again she thought it: *alive*, and the people inside were doing its bidding.

The fifth time she circled back to the courtyard she heard a great clanging and crashing and peered out the window to see the twins at play. They were fencing with stage swords, one of which had a red stain up to the hilt.

"I'll skewer you through the eye socket!" roared Ralf, lunging at his brother. Gail fumbled with his sword and nearly dropped it.

"Never, you . . . you . . . stinking haddock!"

"You *know* that's not the line," Ralf snapped.

"Well, if you won't let me read the script—"

Ralf lurched at Gail, who turned tail and ran. Ralf chased him around the courtyard with the sword.

Sophie turned away, disgusted, and tried to find her way back to the grand entrance hall. Instead she found herself at a dead end crowded with dismantled machinery and whistles from fairground rides. A mechanical horse glared at her, and when she reached out to touch it, its jaw dropped open, revealing nutcracker teeth.

As she turned she heard huge, wracking sobs that bubbled out of the walls like ghosts. Disturbed, she looked around. It was coming from somewhere above her, drifting through layers of plaster and thickened to a muffled bleat.

Sophie drifted toward the crying, losing and picking the sound up again like a thread. The house was riddled with unused rooms. Some were crawling with slugs and snails, and others hid birds' nests and families of mice. The air was strung with the constant clamor of seagulls and the breaking of waves, and the occasional unearthly moan from the water below. Sometimes it felt like she was bypassing whole floors, the stairs not matching the number of windows visible from the outside. The house was an unmapped world, and she felt like the first human to land there.

Apart from the sobbing, which had stopped again, Sophie had no idea what she was looking for. She scanned every inch of the walls as she climbed, trying to grab the weird sensation of familiarity she'd felt when she saw the stair banisters last night.

At the very end of the last hallway was a door with a polished handle. The carpet outside it was red, the algae trodden away by ceaseless pacing. The handle turned easily, and Sophie stepped inside.

She walked into a treasure trove—a cave of tapestries and clothes and jewelry, of bronze lamps and heavy furniture. The ceiling dripped with expensive scarves and moth-eaten furs. The smell of perfume was so heavy it made Sophie's nose ache. She glanced around, then buried her face in a polar bear coat.

It was clear that someone lived here. It felt like the room

was waiting for them to come back. She went to the dressing table, which was covered in bottles and unraveling doilies. She hesitatingly touched the mirror, leaving deep, dusty fingerprints.

On the dressing table was a stack of paper, held down by a lump of rock. Each piece seemed to have been torn from the front of a book, or was part of a ripped-up flour bag or ancient newspaper. She slid a handful out and began to read.

"I am running away. I am going to London to make my fortune. I hope you rot here."

She frowned and flipped to the next one which said, in a different hand:

"Good-bye. By the time you read this, I will be gone. I have left to start a better life."

Another: *"I'm leaving now. Say good-bye to the twins for me. Worst wishes."*

And the next. And the next. All of them short, written in a cramped hand, scribbled fast.

Sophie reasoned they must be from the other servants the twins mentioned. She felt a quick burst of hope. There were people here before her, and they got away! *Or they tried to*, a nasty voice said in the back of her head. *There's nothing to say they actually made it.*

She pushed her doubt away and looked around the room. A hanging scarf brushed the top of her head like a hand and made her shudder.

With the notes still in her grasp she slid open the drawers under the dresser. But the back of her neck tingled. She felt like someone was breathing behind her.

Sophie turned around in time to see a mound of white detach itself from the wall. It sailed across the room with a huge, terrifying face, and roared so loudly the papers went flying. Sophie dodged away from the creature and saw a mountain of red hair, eyes puffed up from weeping, and a dress so voluminous it must have had scaffolding beneath to support it. This thing—this woman—had tiny, slippered feet which despite her apparent weight were noiseless. Sophie's memory connected with the thing in front of her. *The Battleship.*

She tried to gather the papers that had fled across the carpet, but the woman's doughy hand grabbed the back of her neck and hauled her up.

"Who are you? Are you spying on me?"

Sophie shook her head, hanging two inches above the floor. The Battleship's face filled her vision.

"Can't breathe . . ." she said.

"Well?"

"I'm . . . the new . . . girl."

"Another one? They keep sending me servants with no manners. What were you going to take?"

"Nothing," she gasped. "I got lost." The woman dropped her.

"And you thought looking at my things would help you." The Battleship glanced at the papers, then ground one under her foot. "You're an abysmal thief. They're not worth anything."

Sophie winced, waiting for the slippered foot to jab her in the ribs. But nothing happened. "Who wrote them?"

"The twittering girls and boys that come to help the General," the Battleship said. "They get everything they need, food and a bed, and what do they do? They run away in the night and leave their stupid little notes—'*I'm going to be famous.*'" Her voice wavered in mockery. "I blame it on Cartwright. It always seems to happen after his visits."

The woman turned to her dresser and unscrewed a tube of mauve lipstick.

"I'm sorry to have disturbed you, Battl—your ladyship," Sophie said.

"You're not sorry," the woman said, not looking away. "What do you want, if you're not going to steal anything?"

"I was looking for . . . I don't know. Nothing."

"Then go away."

Sophie opened the door to slip out, but before she did curiosity got the better of her.

"Why were you crying?" she asked.

The Battleship only stared at her, lipstick hovering halfway to her face, like Sophie had spoken in a different language. Perhaps nobody had asked her that before.

"Why is your hair white?" she asked back.

"I was left in the snow when I was a baby," said Sophie, then closed the door and fled.

Chapter 5

Cartwright Is Coming

Sophie stood on the flat, gray beach at the back of the house, hidden in the shadow of a fifty-foot cliff. The house stood on top of it, leering with its glassy eyes, spitting bits of rubble as the sound of the lunchtime feeding bell slowly died away.

Scree crunched through pebbles and sea glass and soft pieces of driftwood to thrust a sack into her hand, but Sophie was too preoccupied with the view to notice.

"I remember now," she said. "This house was famous when I was younger. I *knew* I'd seen the carvings before."

Scree grunted in affirmation. She looked at the hundreds upon hundreds of wooden frames sticking out of the water. They looked like dining tables on long legs. Age had turned them gray and black and green, and they stretched for miles through the water, with holes in the spindly forest where a creature had broken through. It was an oyster farm, left to rack and ruin.

"We were rich once," said Scree. "We had fifty people working for us. Everyone ate our oysters."

"We had them for tea," Sophie remembered. Gray, slimy things like blobs of phlegm. She would hide them in the potted palm at dinner. Her parents thought eating tinned oysters was a sign of good breeding, but she'd quickly decided that they were only pretending to like them.

"The oyster farm was a stroke of genius on his lordship's part, rest his creaking old soul," said Scree. "Nobody wanted the old island, but the oysters loved it, and people love oysters. So he bought it and made his fortune selling tinned shellfish."

Sophie remembered that there had been a picture on the tin—an oyster leaping over a rainbow-covered island, apples hanging from trees. She'd made a slingshot and used the tins for target practice.

"What happened to them?" she asked.

"They ran out. The monsters sniffed 'em from miles away and used it like a buffet table. When the oysters disappeared the monsters stayed, then they started tearing up the island until I had the idea of feeding 'em. It's a partnership."

"The man in the portrait. He was the twins' dad, wasn't he? Oyster farm man."

"His name was *Laurel*," Scree said, frowning at her. "He was nearly as good an oyster farmer as he was an inventor. You see that?" He pointed at a large, rusty machine facedown on the beach. "It shells oysters, that does. Nearly took my fingers off once."

"What happened to Laurel?"

"He got depressed when the oyster business went under. He was never a happy soul. I discovered him on the beach one day, drowned and frozen solid with icicles hanging from his nose. Right where you're standing now, in fact."

Sophie took a step to the right.

"Anyway," said Scree, "when the water froths, throw the food as hard as you can. All at once. Then run."

He hurried back to the catacombs. Sophie untied the sack, trying not to look inside. She heard a distant rumbling and gritted her teeth.

"Come and get it," she said, mostly to herself.

There was a deep roar and water rolled over the beach, making every stone tremble. She flung the bag toward the sea and its contents flew out, landing across the water in an arc. But instead of running she found herself rooted to the spot, watching the waves slapping at the oyster racks, and it wasn't until something long and green heaved from the water that she sprinted away.

A tentacle hit the ground behind her with such force that she fell over. She saw Scree pick up his grab-claw contraption, presumably to chase the creature away, but the tentacle grabbed her foot and flipped her onto her back.

"Don't you dare!" she yelled, and grabbing a stone brought it down on the tentacle as hard as she could. She opened her mouth to scream, but all the breath was knocked from her lungs and she rattled over the beach like she was being dragged by a car.

Suddenly the monster let her go with a snap of its tentacle. Seizing her chance, Sophie scrambled back up the beach on her hands and knees, waiting for it to come back and get a better grip on her. But it didn't. She heard a low, sonorous moan from under the water, and an answering cry, then the creature reared up, sniffed like a dog, and dived so fast a wave crashed over her head.

"What was that?" she cried, swerving into the entrance of the catacombs.

"That was your lucky break," said Scree, not looking remotely concerned about her welfare. "They found something better to have a go at."

"Oh, goody," she said, wringing her hair out.

"There's only one thing they'd give up fresh meat for, and it's the one thing they've never been able to catch. The flea in the proverbial earhole."

"The what?"

"Cartwright is coming," he said darkly.

"Cartwright," she repeated. The person she'd been waiting for. She was curious to know just how this person was going to reach the island despite there being no path and a pack of furious monsters between him and the shore.

The twins and the Battleship stood in front of the house, waiting, almost invisible in the gloom. Ralf and Gail were pinching each other. Their mother wasn't blinking, and may as well have been stuffed for display except that her nostrils flared every so often.

Sophie stood behind them, deep in the Battleship's shadow.

"Who's Cartwright?" she asked Scree, who was gripping his pocket watch like a talisman.

Scree pressed his lips together.

"I know you can hear me. I'll keep asking until you answer."

Scree sucked his teeth and cracked his lips open, just slightly.

62

"Cartwright is the Battleship's nephew. He was taken in five years ago, 'cause his parents died of the Sea Fever."

"They died of it?"

"They went mad and threw themselves off a cliff. Thought they were being chased by a crab. Turns out it was the neighbor's Border terrier. Then he came here. Really took to Laurel. Didn't get on with anyone else, though."

"Surprising," Sophie said drily, looking at the twins. "And . . . he just left again?"

"Joined the army when Laurel died. He was only twelve. They must've been desperate."

"Clearly."

The Battleship swung her body around, like a boat pulling into the harbor, to scowl at Sophie.

Sophie shut her mouth and fixed her gaze on the sea. When the Battleship's eyes glazed over again she whispered, "Would he have contacts on the New Continent?"

"Prob'ly."

"What does he do in the army?"

"How should I know?" Scree muttered, irritated, and plucked an errant snail from the wall of the house.

The twins, bored of tormenting each other, were now staring into the middle distance with their mouths faintly twitching like they were solving equations. Sophie noticed that Gail had a nervous tic, his fingers curling and uncurling like they were on strings. His brother, though—

"Stop thinking about us," Ralf said.

Sophie's head jerked back toward the sea.

Silence fell. The sea changed color as the night eased in. The sea creatures must have smelled Cartwright coming from a long way off, unless they'd already eaten him. Still, better him than her, Sophie thought.

A chill began to set in, and her fingers slowly turned numb. She wondered if they'd be out there all night.

"Right at the last minute," Scree muttered scornfully, pointing a crooked finger at the sea.

And there he was.

A dot on the horizon, plowing toward them through sheets of foam. The drumming of hoofs against rock, a spray of gulls and squawks and feathers.

There was a boy on a horse, and the horse was running over the sea.

Leaping over the waves, legs skittering and bending like pieces of rubber, the horse and its rider galloped toward them. There was a monstrous roar that made Scree wince, and another, and another, merging into a cacophony of noise until the water was a thrashing, heaving mess of black slime and saucer-shaped eyes.

The dot grew into blue and red and gold, and all of that turned into a body and a face, and suddenly Cartwright was upon them.

The horse was big and black and had hooves like dinner plates. It leaped from sea creature to sea creature, crashing down on one globulous head after the other, dancing through tentacled loops and gnashing its teeth at whatever got in its way. Bits of jelly, lumps of furious monster-flesh, flew from the surface of the water. Sophie couldn't imagine how the rider wasn't being thrown off, but then she saw the horse's mad eyes and the foam flying from its mouth, and realized that Cartwright was basically insane.

The horse and its rider plowed through the jagged rocks, knocking so many of them into the water that Scree gave a moan, and Sophie put her hand on his shoulder before remembering that those things nearly ripped her to shreds.

As they flew toward the island the boy on the horse drew his sword, and without looking swung it over his head, chopping off a tentacle that was about to grab his throat. Then the horse leaped from the rocks, tore through the shrubbery, landed, and reared in front of the twins, screeching through gravestone teeth. Its body twisted in the middle before crashing down on the ground. Water splattered from under its hooves, and from the pile of dark hair and gnashing teeth emerged its rider.

Sophie noticed his boots first. They were the kind of boots that people who are in charge wear.

"Hello, Cartwright," Ralf mumbled as the horse writhed at his feet. "Don't you look different."

"Hello, Cartwright," muttered Gail.

As Cartwright stepped into the light Sophie could see his uniform, which was royal blue and red with gold piping and brass buttons. He towered over all of them, beaming widely, and there was something very much like the twins about him. He had the same red hair, and that thin, overstretched face, with eerily pale eyes. You could say he was handsome, Sophie thought, if you enjoyed being terrified all the time.

The sea churned, and a jellyfish the size of a large dog surfaced in the broil, bringing a smell of mulch and rotting vegetables. The jellyfish, which had a starfish embedded in its side, washed into the garden, flailing and convulsing. Before anyone could move it swept past the horse and the twins, whose mouths were hanging open like fishing nets, and came right for Sophie.

It skimmed toward her on a crest of water, its venomous tentacles trailing behind it like bits of old rope. Sophie leaped away just before it reached her, and it hit the wall behind her instead. The water swept back again, pulling the jellyfish with it, right into the mouth of a waiting creature. Oozing satisfaction, the creature sank back into the water. There was a horseshoe-shaped print on its head.

Cartwright didn't say anything for a few seconds. He hadn't looked at Sophie once. And then, very elegantly, he yawned.

"You still have the monster problem, then."

The Battleship threw her head back and laughed so hard her body shook. Then she stopped abruptly as though a cork had been put in her throat.

"Nothing's changed since your last visit," she said.

"The twins haven't made it to London yet?"

"No."

"Shame. I do so love their performances."

Sophie snorted with laughter, then stuffed her fingers in her mouth. Nobody saw. She might as well have been invisible.

"What's wrong with the horse?" Gail asked. He went to poke it with his foot, and withdrew when its great yellow teeth snapped down on his laces.

"He's happy to see you," said Cartwright. "Scree, put him away, won't you?"

With that he marched to the doors, flung them open, and disappeared. The twins glanced at each other and ran after him.

"Ladyship . . . its teeth . . . you won't make me, will you?" Scree said. "It'll chew my fingers off!"

"Do as he says, General," the Battleship barked. Then she looked at Sophie. "Let the girl help. She could do with a scaring."

She went into the house. The horse chopped its teeth together with the noise of a guillotine. Neither of its eyes were focused in the same direction.

"It looks manic," Sophie said.

"That's its name," Scree said bitterly. "Manic the horse. It's even carved in the bottom of its horseshoes, which you'll see when it tries to kick you."

Sophie knew horses like that; they were born with a temper, couldn't be trained, and often ended up being made into glue. They were huge and surly and sometimes deadly . . . if you didn't know what you were doing.

Sophie went forward, chest tightening, and put her hand on Manic's nose. She winced, but Manic just *har-rumphed* and looked sour.

"Watch out," said Scree. "It's trying to look innocent. Give it a chance and it'll be over the horizon before you can blink."

"I know," Sophie replied, and despite the pain in her arm she smiled to herself.

A horse like this could be useful.

Chapter 6

Dinner Is Served

When they had wrestled Manic into the stables and bolted the door—twice—Sophie went back to the house, keeping her distance from the shore, where the creatures gurgled and grumbled. She followed the sound of conversation to a dining room at the back of the house, where there was a table set for twenty, each place bordered by enough knives, forks, and spoons for a ten-course meal. She slid into the room and stood in a corner. She wanted to get a better look at the new arrival.

Cartwright was sharpening his butter knife with his back to the door, sitting opposite the twins, who were staring at him with barely disguised hatred. The Battleship was at the head of the table, ensconced on a wooden throne decorated with unusually vicious-looking mermaids.

The room was cavernous. On the ceiling, plaster cherubim were surrounded by fields of real, gravity-defying mushrooms, and bronze oysters tangled with living ivy on the walls. Streamers of brown who-knows-what hung from the ceiling among ropes of mussels. On the wall beside her was a damp, framed advertisement for Laurel's Golden Oysters. She looked at the painting of dancing shells and the dubious claim that they were "The Happiest Shellfish from the Freshest Sea," then back at the table. She'd always suspected that advertisments were a load of rubbish.

"What are we having?" Ralf asked loudly.

"I hope it's roast beef," said Gail. "I like it black and crunchy."

"With peas like bullets."

"And bloody gravy."

"Fish," said the Battleship abruptly. They all looked at her. "Just like last night, and the night before. We're drowning in fish. How do you even know about roast beef?"

"We read about it," Ralf said. "People eat it in London."

"The girl would know," said Gail. "She's from London, isn't she?"

The twins fixed their eyes on Sophie. She'd thought she was invisible.

"The new girl should sit with us," Ralf said. "Wouldn't that be nice, Gail?"

"Definitely," said Gail.

The Battleship shifted her body in the great throne, which creaked like a tree in high wind.

"I don't trust her," she announced. "Have you seen the way she looks at things? Like she's working out how to steal them. I don't like it one bit."

"I'm not trying to steal anything," Sophie said coldly.

"That's what a thief would say," said the Battleship.

"Shut up, Mother," Ralf said, and they instantly forgot about Sophie. "It's too early to start with all that. Cartwright's only been here a minute."

"Be quiet," said the Battleship. "I can't stand your whining."

"Here we go," said Gail smugly. "'I wish you'd died when your father did,' blah blah blah."

"Except we *didn't*," Ralf said. "And we're your sons."

"You should look after us. You should love us."

"Instead you float around weeping and moaning about Father."

"You never liked him when he was alive."

"You weren't very nice to him. Maybe he drowned out of spite."

"Enough!" the Battleship roared, slamming her fork on the table so hard it bent in two. The twins looked pleased with themselves.

In the flat silence that followed, Cartwright cleared his throat.

"I love fish," he said. "Particularly the special way Scree makes it, all dry and crusty in a way nobody else can. It's the most unforgettable part of my childhood."

"Your *childhood*," snorted Ralf. "Listen to you, all grown up. Just because you're fourteen. Just because you're in the *army*. How did you get in, anyway?"

"They made an exception to the age limit as soon as they saw me," said Cartwright.

"Were they taking in stray cats, too?" said Ralf.

Cartwright's hand tightened around his butter knife.

"We're practicing a play we wrote," interrupted Gail. "I'm ever so good at acting."

"I'm brilliant at acting, too," said Ralf.

"I can see," said Cartwright. "The talent is just pouring off you. What is your play about?"

"A mad queen and her mad son and her dead husband," said Gail promptly. "And another mad girl, can't remember who *she* is, but she drowns herself in a river. Or a bathtub, I don't know. There's a skull in it and everything. It's ever so funny."

"What a fantastic story," said Cartwright.

"When we take it to London it's sure to be a hit. We'll have money pouring out of our noses."

"Undoubtedly."

"It's extremely moving. We'll show it to you after dinner."

"I'd enjoy that very much."

There was a pause. The twins looked at Cartwright suspiciously.

"Really?"

"No," said Cartwright. "I'd rather die."

"We used to like you," snarled Ralf. "You were so *stupid*. We could stick your head in the toilet and all you'd do was blubber."

"And now," said Cartwright, "I'd tear your silly little heads off. You see, while you've been here skulking in the dark, I've been clubbing people over the head with bayonets. I no longer find you intimidating, although I *do* have the urge to hang you out the window by your ankles. Luckily," he added pleasantly, "I have also learned the art of tolerance, and may be able to restrain myself."

The twins gaped at him. Ralf turned an alarming shade of red.

"Do we have any presents from overseas?" Gail asked hopefully.

"No. I was fighting."

"Didn't you have holidays?" asked Ralf.

"This," said Cartwright, "*is* my holiday, wretched as it is."

Sophie was beginning to like Cartwright, despite the fact that he insisted on acting so much older than them all. She'd almost forgotten that she was eavesdropping until the twins turned their gazes toward her again.

"Thing!" called Ralf, making Sophie jump. "Come and sit down."

"Learn my name first," she snapped.

"You're rude. We should hold your head under the faucet," said Ralf, picking up his cutlery.

"Ooh, nasty," said Gail.

"Would you like that fork in your head?" she said. And there it was—the thing that kept getting her into trouble. She couldn't help it. If anyone prodded her she had to attack, even if she knew she'd regret it later. She forced herself to uncurl her hand, which had formed a fist.

"She looks so strange, doesn't she?" said Ralf to Gail.

"Sort of like one of those things that lives in the bathtub."

"A slither-fish," said Gail.

"Silverfish," Sophie corrected automatically. The twins hooted with laughter.

"Silverfish! Silverfish! Stamp on the silverfish!"

Sophie was halfway across the room, ready to leap across the table and hit them, when Scree burst in with their food. With the twins' attention distracted, Cartwright grabbed Sophie's shoulder and pushed her into a chair.

She was so surprised that she sat down immediately. Cartwright smiled mildly.

"Don't you just love a hot meal?" he said. "I was so hungry today I almost had to eat my boots."

Scree slammed down a huge silver platter holding a fat, curled-up fish with a foot-long fork sticking from its head, a bowl of floury potatoes, and some damp lumps of vegetable. He scuttled out and came back with more. A bucket of gray sauce. A dessert made almost entirely of pale custard. As soon as he swung the dishes down onto the table, the twins grabbed things with their long fingers, piling their plates high and licking their hands. They poured glasses of gravy, strained the sauce between their teeth, and packed the vegetables into tight balls and flicked them away from their plates.

"Fish?" Cartwright asked Sophie pleasantly. Before she could answer, Cartwright picked up the serving tongs and reached for it. Ralf whipped the fish away and tipped most of it onto his own plate.

"I wasn't hungry anyway," said Sophie as her stomach moaned.

Scree hobbled off and came back with juice. As soon as it was on the table the twins poured it into their mouths, dribbling it down their fronts and staining their chins purple. It was doubtful that much of it had reached their stomachs, but the effort involved was mesmerizing. It was like watching pigs at the zoo.

"Why do you have the misfortune of being here?" Cartwright asked Sophie without looking at her.

"Stop talking," snapped Gail, kicking Sophie under the table so hard she yelped. "Ralf, they're talking about us."

Ralf lobbed a spoon at Cartwright's head. Cartwright dodged casually, and it sailed over his shoulder.

When the fish had been consumed the twins started throwing potatoes at each other, while the Battleship silently vacuumed fish flesh from the bone. Sophie looked just in time to see Ralf and Gail wink at each other. She ducked and a potato sailed over her head. Scree, who was miserably standing by the wall, raised a dish to his face and narrowly missed being blinded by a sprout.

"Ten points!" screamed Ralf.

"Twelve!" screeched Gail.

"Shut up!" The Battleship, having finished her food, rose and threw a plate at her sons, who ducked and laughed as it shattered behind them. Decorative shellfish fell from the wall in clouds of dust. Sophie bowed her head and grabbed her fork, and the fight began.

Food traveled like cannon fire between the twins and their mother, tight clumps of potato and gravy thickening the air and turning the surface of the table into a slurry. Cartwright caught a flying chunk of gray bread and started eating it quickly, bowing his head to let a cup sail past. Sophie turned her plate over and held it in front of her face seconds before something hit it. Insults flew between the twins and their mother as fast as the airborne food, the twins punctuating their tirade with horrible, theatrical laughter.

Cartwright concentrated on his bread with a practiced ferocity.

"Grab what you can before the twins snatch it, or you'll starve," he said.

"I'm pretty sure that bread is made from fish gristle," Sophie said, but she was so hungry she ducked from her chair and grabbed some from the floor anyway. She stuffed it into her mouth and swallowed nearly without chewing, her stomach singing with relief.

When she'd finished she weighed her options: She could try to make friends with Cartwright, or avoid suspicion by making herself as inconspicuous as possible. In the end, her curiosity won out.

"Have the twins always been like this?" she said, knowing they couldn't hear her over their own screaming.

"Always. Don't be fooled, though. They act like idiots but they're really rather clever. They once made a jack-in-the-box that looked exactly like me, then wound it up and left it outside my door. I jumped so hard I gave myself a black eye."

"I'll look out for mysterious boxes, then."

For some reason this made Cartwright grin.

"What's your name?" he asked, putting his bread down. She hesitated. But maybe it didn't matter if he knew.

"Sophie."

"I'm Master Most Violent Cartwright. Really. My parents thought it was funny."

"STOP HAVING FUN!" Ralf screamed at them, going purple in the face. He grabbed one of the gravy boats and flung its contents at his cousin.

Without looking up, Cartwright drew a pistol from the inside of his jacket and shot a hole through the gravy boat, which was still in Ralf's hand. The room fell into dripping silence. Only the curtains moved, driven by a breeze from the sea.

"Whoops," said Cartwright. "Silly me. I'm afraid I lost my manners in the army."

"That was my favorite gravy boat!" the Battleship snapped, breaking the spell. "You nasty little *idiots*!" She slammed her cutlery onto the table and swooped out, leaving a trail of broken crockery.

"Having fun, Silverfish?" Ralf asked as Gail wheezed with laughter. "It's only just beginning."

She looked right back at him and said, "So am I."

Cartwright neatly dabbed his chin with a napkin and strolled out without a word. The twins grinned at each other, wiped their fingers under the table, and followed him.

"Nighty-night, Silverfish," leered Ralf.

"Nighty-night, Silverfish," sang Gail.

When they had all gone Sophie got up and started to scrape mush out of her hair. Scree appeared beside her, fish sauce running down the side of his head.

"That went well," he said. "I didn't give 'em real knives this time. See how much you can scrape off the walls, and I'll fetch the mop."

She limped around the room, staring at the lumps of food smeared everywhere. She hadn't asked Cartwright about his horse or worked out where he kept the key for the stable. Her eyes flicked to the door. Scree would probably be gone for a while anyway.

She abandoned the dining room and ran up the corridor in Cartwright's direction. She swerved into the entrance hall and cursed. Everyone had left.

"You're wondering what just happened, aren't you," Cartwright's voice said in her ear. "Don't worry. You'll get used to it."

Sophie turned and stamped on his toe, hard. She didn't even think about it. Cartwright gave a squeak of pain.

"What was that for?" he asked.

"You made me jump," she said, breathing again.

"Most people would scream."

"Most people are idiots. You shouldn't sneak up on anyone."

"I wasn't sneaking. The carpet muffled the sound of my footsteps."

She looked down at his black boots and thought that it was very unlikely. There was something about Cartwright that she couldn't quite put her finger on, but it wasn't pleasant.

"You were waiting for me," she said. "What do you want?"

"You were following me. What do *you* want?"

"I asked first."

Cartwright shrugged, wearing an infuriating smile. He withdrew a fork from his pocket and started playing with it, twisting the prongs out of shape.

Don't give in, Sophie told herself.

He yawned.

"What do you want?" she exploded.

"Nothing. How long have you been here?" he asked.

"A day."

"Do you like adventures?"

"I like telling stories. I'm a storyteller," she said, then realized she'd told him too much. "Why are *you* here?"

"A holiday. And a task. Do you want to get off this island?" he said.

She looked at him sharply.

"I can get you out of here," he said. "And more. I can get you a ticket to the New Continent."

She snorted. He sounded like one of those dodgy traveling salesmen that offer genuine antelope-skin jackets for the price of a fish.

"Why is that funny?" he asked, looking annoyed.

"Because there's no way you have a ticket. Anyway, why would you help me?"

"I feel sorry for anyone who's stuck in this madhouse," he said, putting on a decent impression of being hurt. "I had to live here for the most miserable years of my life. Nobody deserves *that*."

"I want to know what the catch is," she said.

"Well . . . you might be able to do me a small favor. I need you to find something for me."

Find something. How wonderfully vague.

"I won't do it," she said.

"You don't even know what it is. It's very exciting."

"And what makes you think you can trust me?"

"Nothing yet," he said. "But you said that you're a storyteller. So let me get to know you. Spin me a tale."

Sophie looked around. The entrance hall was empty but for the slow drip of water, and Scree was nowhere to be seen. Stories were something she could do. And that would show him, wouldn't it? He'd see how clever she really was.

"All right," she said. "I'll tell you a story."

"What's it about?"

"It's about a girl and a fish."

He nodded. She picked up a fish skeleton from the floor, letting it swing gently by the tail, and looking into its snowy rib cage she began.

Chapter 7

The Queen of the Sea

In Which Nobody Is Fooled by a Generous Offer

In a cave at the top of the world, where the Arctic mountains touch the sky, an old man and an old woman dug themselves a home in the ice. They had a child, and they called her Fishmoth.

Fishmoth was not afraid of the snow, or the dark, or of the great white creatures that stalked the ice fields. Her hair was so cold it was transparent like glass, and her skin was as thin as a sheet of frost. When she walked into snowstorms she became invisible, but she never got lost.

One day Fishmoth was sitting in her cave when she saw a traveler. He told her the story of the crown of the sea, which would make its wearer a queen, and in return asked for water.

But when she gave it to him it froze in her hands, and when he put it to his mouth he grew so cold he died.

Fishmoth's parents, horrified by her power, waited until she was asleep and sealed her in the cave behind a sheet of ice. When she woke up they were long gone. She was so angry she smashed the ice down with her bare fists.

She stepped over the body of the frozen traveler and walked south.

She walked for days and weeks and months. The stars began to look different, the air became warmer, and the trees and the earth changed color. She climbed mountains, and as the air warmed, she melted. Her lips became pink, her hands cracked, and her hair turned into a sheet of water. She trickled down the other side of the mountains and landed in a brook.

A brown fish rose from the brook and said:

"I will swallow you and take you to the South Sea inside my cool belly, and there I will spit you out and you can take your crown, whereupon you will be the queen of the sea and the sun will never bother you again. In return, bring me the jewel that is lost at the bottom of my stomach."

Fishmoth agreed and the fish swallowed her. Searching his dark stomach with her hands, she found the stone immediately. But there were other things in there—hairpins, and bones, and *three small teeth. She shuddered when she realized what the fish had done, and what he was planning for her.*

Fishmoth held the stone and waited. She and the fish traveled far together, and when they reached the South Sea the fish spat her out, and she emerged with the red, fist-sized jewel.

As the brown fish rejoiced she struck it over the head with the red stone, so swiftly that it died without noticing. The fish split open, and out came the remains of all the queens it had treacherously eaten, which she buried under a juniper tree in a silk handkerchief.

Fishmoth used the stone to weigh herself down and dropped to the bottom of the sea to where the crown lay. She put it on and swam back to the surface, the beautiful red stone in her pocket.

Now she was the queen of the sea, revered by the creatures that lived in it, and she remained that way for the earth's eternity, all the way until the sun went out.

Chapter 8

Manic the Horse

Sophie, sleeping crookedly on her stone slab, dreamed of being the queen of the sea. She fell under the waves and the creatures heaved her out again, and when she emerged she had a crown made of bicycle spokes and seaweed and a cloak made of locked-together crabs. The loose ribbons of the dream-story swirled round and round until one got caught on the back of her eyelid and slowly, gently, tugged her awake.

Her mouth tasted like old leather and her spine was stiff from being bent by the hard bed. For a while she stared into the clammy darkness of night, wondering why she'd told that story to Cartwright when she'd sworn she wouldn't let anything out of her head.

But this wasn't the time for regrets. She had an escape plan to carry out, and she needed to do it before morning.

She rolled out of bed, felt her way into her clothes and shoes, and walked blindly through the catacombs toward the stale breathing of the house.

Cartwright's bedroom was near the twins' room of destruction, opposite a particularly bad painting of snow-struck mountains. She knew because she'd followed him there earlier. He'd gone a very strange route—it was almost like he was trying to make sure nobody could keep track of him—but then he'd arrived and shut himself in.

It was the work of minutes to quietly break the lock with a fork. Cartwright slept like a corpse. He was laid out neatly on top of the bedsheets, still fully dressed, with his arms by his sides and his chin pointed at the ceiling. His skin looked white and cold, and only the faint twitch of his eyelids said that he was still alive. His hair looked as though it had collected dust in the brief time he'd been here. Cartwright was, she thought, hideously unattractive.

First she needed to find the tickets. She crouched to look under the bed, but saw only boots and a small tin of shoe polish. Then she went to the chest of drawers and opened them one by one. There were two pairs of socks, a comb with razor-sharp teeth that looked like a weapon, and a crumpled map of Portsmouth. Nothing else. She felt a twinge of disappointment before noticing a piece of paper sticking out from the lining of the drawer, and with some careful tweaking managed to get it out.

It was an envelope, thin and grubby, and inside—yes! She slid the tickets out. They were thin and crackly, covered in gold leaf and spidery black writing. She tilted one toward the light.

HB Victoria Steam Cruisers
presents
Your one-way ticket to the New Continent.
Over 300 ships departing for certain paradise
~ Twice a week from five ports until boats run out! ~

She felt suddenly disappointed. She'd never seen a ticket up close, and knowing this was what her parents got rid of her for was almost humiliating. They were like the tokens you'd buy at a fun fair in exchange for rides. Her fingers twitched with the impulse to tear them into confetti.

Before she could do any damage she thrust one into her pocket and dumped the other on top of the dresser. Next she searched behind the curtains and around the bed until she found Cartwright's sword. She swung it a couple of times, almost smashing a lamp. She might have to hurt some people on her way to Portsmouth. Anyone who hadn't already fled the country for the New Continent would be desperate and probably mad with Sea Fever, and she didn't want to be an easy target.

As she lowered the sword she noticed a short length of cord hanging from the side of the bed and disappearing under Cartwright's pillow. She smiled. It was too easy.

"You're an idiot," she informed him, and slid the key to the stables out. She wound the cord around her wrist, walked backward out of the room, and bowed.

"Thank you, Most Violent," she said. "It's been a pleasure."

Then she ran, dragging the sword behind her, fleeing through the house like a ghost, slipping through a small window on the ground floor and landing outside in a bed of thistles. The ocean was flat and calm, the air still. She jogged down to the stables, where through the five-inch-thick door she could hear Manic shuffling his hooves.

She unbolted the door and forced the key into the lock. It swung open, and moonlight flooded in. There were twelve stalls inside, and Manic was standing in two of them.

"Hello, Manic," she said, and held out her hand as she walked toward him. He was even bigger than she remembered, and doubt bobbed to the surface like an ice cube.

"I bet you don't like being cooped up in here. Would you like to go for a ride?"

He regarded her with his yellow eyes, and with a long, deliberate *crunch* he crushed a plank of wood between his teeth.

"Right," she said. "You're hungry. I should have brought food. But there are lots of fish in the sea, and you can have as many as you want. Won't that be nice?"

He spat out the piece of wood. She went over and patted his nose, which was somewhere above her head. He shuffled his feet, then nudged her so hard she fell over backward.

"I'll take that as yes," she said, and unhooked the saddle from the wall, making sure not to break eye contact with him. "I'm just going to put this nice comfy seat on you."

Manic swung his head around, tugged the saddle from her hands, and sat down on it. He snorted. If she didn't know any better she'd say he was laughing at her. She stepped back. His yellow eyes fixed themselves on her like fog lamps, waiting for her next move.

"I get it," she said. "It's a game. That's fine. I'll do without the saddle."

She climbed over the piles of broken wood, and he gnashed at her as soon as she was within biting distance. Then he stopped. Out at sea, something was stirring. Sophie could hear the sucking of the waves, and looking out the door she saw a gray tentacle rise from the water.

Manic whinnied excitedly and got to his feet so quickly Sophie backed into a corner to stop herself being crushed. He cantered out of the stable and into the garden, crushing stones beneath his colossal feet, as the tentacle waved to him like a flag.

"You mean you *like* stamping on sea creatures?" she said, then, realizing what was about to happen, grabbed her sword and took off after him, jumping over piles of fallen brick and dodging broken statues. By the edge of the garden Manic had broken into a full-blown gallop. The tentacle in the sea was joined by another and another, on and on until a forest of slime was gyrating above the waves. And Manic wasn't slowing down.

"Stop!" Sophie yelled. He slowed down to swerve around a tree and got caught in the branches. She caught up and grabbed a handful of his mane, but Manic, now free, had other ideas, and she was dragged along for a couple of yards. "What sort of horse are you?" she cried. Manic shook his huge head, almost knocking her over. Then he drew up beside a garden wall, and taking a chance, she swung herself onto it, balanced on the wall with her toes, and leaped onto Manic's back.

The tentacles disappeared with a splash. Manic sat down.

Fighting a scream of frustration, Sophie dug her feet into his sides. That's what people did to get horses moving, wasn't it?

"You have a serious attitude problem, you know that?" she told Manic. "But I'm not giving up until you've crossed the sea. I've seen you do it. I know it's possible. Get up and start walking, or I'll stay sitting on you all night, no matter how cold or wet I get and no matter how much you complain. I'm in charge and I'm going to win."

Manic started to tear up weeds.

Sophie groaned and buried her face in his mane, which smelled of old socks. Any minute now someone in the house was going to wake up and wonder what was going on. Neptune only knew what they'd do to her when they realized she'd tried to escape. They'd throw her into the sea or mash her up for dinner.

"Hey," she said, looking up. She filled her lungs and started waving her arms at the sea. "CREATURES! IT'S SUPPERTIME!"

She hadn't expected anything to happen, but within

seconds the water started to bubble and a black shadow rose and burst out in a sheet of foam. Manic stood up so quickly her stomach dropped, and she just had time to wind her fists into his mane before he started galloping again. She plunged her hand into her coat and pulled out a bone, which she threw into the water as hard as possible. A stingray with a body the size of a bedsheet rose to consume it, and Manic jumped.

For a second they were flying through the air, and then they were falling hard, and Sophie wondered for a fraction of a second if they would ever land. They hit the stingray. It was like landing on a plastic sheet, and for a terrible moment it felt like they were about to sink right under the water, but Manic had already started to jump again, this time onto a patch of rocks that no person, or any normal horse, could ever reach. The stingray convulsed, rolled up, and disappeared. Manic skidded to a halt, stamping his feet on the tiny island.

She hadn't expected him to stop. Now that they were still, Sophie was faced with the enormity of what was in front of them: a stretch of sea miles long, deep and deadly and teeming with teeth and tentacles. Manic reared, making an unearthly sound from between his teeth, and she clung on for dear life.

"There! Go that way!" she shouted, pointing at another rock in the water which turned out to be something else entirely.

Manic made another leap, narrowly missing a set of brown teeth, and skidded off something dank and slimy. He stumbled forward and slipped into the sea, front legs skittering out in front of him. She thought they were done for, but then they landed on a submerged rock, the water sloshing up to Sophie's knees.

This was such a bad idea, stupid stupid stupid—

But there was no turning back now.

"Keep going!" she said desperately, digging her knees into Manic's sides. "We have to move!"

Manic stamped and lost his footing on the wet rock, stumbling toward the water. He hit another cluster of rocks and twisted sideways. Gray tentacles arched over them, drawing themselves in like a noose, until Sophie slashed at them with the sword. They screamed inhumanly, then slammed back into the water.

Manic reared again, and she finally slipped off, still clutching his black mane. Her feet were hanging just above the water when a jellyfish rose and spread out beneath her. It was huge and pale blue, and she could see its internal organs contracting and expanding, its huge beating heart and its packed-up stomach writhing. She knew that if she touched it she'd be killed. The creatures in the sea started to jostle for position, smelling a victory, and a squid reached out for Manic . . .

. . . Who turned around and flung himself into the water again. Sophie drew her legs up and just missed the jelly-fish. They were standing on another submerged platform, some old jetty or pier full of holes, and Manic had his head just clear of the waves, dragging her along. She brandished the sword at the things coming toward her. They had no shape or form, only colors and noises and eyes and suckers and shells and gelatinous skins. Something shot through the surface of the water like a rocket, and Sophie stabbed it until it withdrew with an awful cry, an inky substance trailing after it.

Sophie couldn't drag herself back onto Manic. Still holding on to his mane, she started to kick. And then she saw the tall figure in an army uniform standing at the edge of the garden, watching with pale blue eyes.

She opened her mouth to curse and water flooded in. She let go of Manic but not the sword, and immediately started to sink, kicking without effect. On the way down she grabbed one of the pointed rocks that protected the island and dragged herself back up. When the salt cleared from her eyes she knew that she couldn't claw her way back. Manic was gone, and her worst nightmare was in front of her.

She'd never seen a sea creature this close before. She now suspected that her parents were right to be scared. The two eyes in front of her, set deep in a flat, scaled head, were empty and unthinking. It didn't care who she was or why she was there. She was about to be killed by a swimming vegetable.

It reached out a long arm and curled it around her shoulder like it was embracing her. Then it tangled its arm into her hair and peeled her away from the rock like a sea snail.

Sophie took a huge breath and tried to think. She was being dragged backward and under. The sword was too big to lift. And it was cold, dark, weirdly heavy under the water.

She started to grow light-headed. Was this what drowning felt like? It was slow and nasty and claustrophobic. Her brain sent her a message and she started kicking again, but her limbs were heavy and the creature was wrapping itself around her. It hummed a slow, mournful death tune as it started to squeeze.

She knew it wouldn't last long. If she opened her mouth

and sucked the water in, she'd be dead in half a minute. She remembered hearing that you pass out before you drown, which meant it couldn't really hurt. Her hand loosened on the hilt of the sword.

And then something grabbed her foot. She vaguely thought that it was too small to be attacking her—maybe it was a killer starfish—but then she realized that it was a hand. It pulled her hard. The tentacles tightened their grip and pulled back. She was being dragged two ways at once. She was about to be torn in two.

This is not how I'm going to finish my life!

With a last burst of fury, she dragged her sword-wielding arm above her face and swung the blade down on the tentacle that had her hair. She missed her own scalp by inches. The blank-eyed monster screamed, recoiled from her body, and shot off, holding a fistful of her hair, which trailed behind it like silver streamers. Sophie dropped the sword and kicked to the surface. The hand holding her foot had let go. She burst through the water and took huge, burning gulps of air, then thrashed toward the garden as the sea creatures howled behind her.

Cartwright was standing in the water. He held out a hand as she came toward him, but she plunged past it. As she dragged herself onto the steep bank that rose into the garden, she heard gunfire and turned to see him with a pistol in his hand, putting bullets through a giant crab.

Manic was in a rose patch, chewing steadily, regarding her with something like hatred. She wanted to be angry at Manic, but it wasn't the horse's fault. She'd ridden him into the sea. She stole him, and took a sword, and rode him right into a death trap, and nearly got them both drowned. And Cartwright . . .

Cartwright was back on the island, dripping onto the ground. His expression was cold.

"You nearly killed my horse," he said. "Never mind that you so kindly left me one of my tickets. I could have waved it like a flag while the monsters swallowed me up and you pranced off to the New Continent like the bloody fairy queen."

"I didn't mean to," she said, and hated it because she sounded like a little kid. "No, that's a lie," she said. "I meant to. I stole your horse and tried to run away. I wish it had worked."

He looked at her like she was mad. She *felt* mad, having been so close to death and having been saved like she was some idiotic damsel in distress.

"I listened to your story, you know," he said. "You might

as well have told me outright that you just take what you want."

"Stop using that self-important voice," she snapped.

"What," he said, "is wrong with you?"

Mortification burned across her face. She didn't know. She was hot and cold and wet and shivery, and it felt like a strip of skin had been torn from her back where the squid-thing had grabbed her. He reached forward and neatly took the wet ticket from her pocket, and she didn't resist.

"Consider this for a while," said Cartwright. "The reason I get across that monster-infested sea is because I know what I want. Horses like Manic respond to a firm hand and a bit of confidence. The reason you made him panic is because you didn't actually want to leave."

"Trust me, I don't want to be here," Sophie said.

"Don't you?" he said. "I made you an offer of freedom. You must wonder what I want you to find in return. Think of the stories. Think what secrets this abysmal, worm-ridden house has. I could tell you things that would make your hair turn three shades whiter. Why is it white, by the way?"

"I sold my soul to the devil," she said promptly. Cartwright looked momentarily impressed. Forcing her chattering teeth together, and hating herself for asking, she said, "What secrets?"

"Murder," he replied, all cool again. "Guilt. Obsession. Inventions beyond your wildest dreams. You said you like stories; you'll want a part in this one."

"I don't."

"It's too late now, anyway," he said. "The deal's off."

He patted Manic on the side and walked off. The horse cast one long, disgusted look at Sophie, and followed.

"You're wrong!" she shouted after him. "I know what I want!"

He didn't reply. They trudged back to the stables, leaving her standing on the garden bank. There was a squelching sound, and she stamped on a tentacle that had crept up behind her. It withdrew with a hiss.

"He's making things up," she told the offending creature. "Isn't he?"

But the truth was, she wasn't entirely sure.

Chapter 9

The Glowfish Pits

Sophie was woken by the breakfast feeding bell, which shook the catacombs so ferociously a stalactite fell down and missed her head by an inch. She yelped and ran to the beach, still wearing nightclothes, crunching through the piles of flotsam. In a panic she grabbed whatever she could find: bones and clumps of seaweed and even things that looked like old clothes heaved up by the sea. She tossed them to the creatures. They took everything, screaming and seething and flinging themselves around so angrily stones fell from the side of the cliff.

Trudging back, Sophie became aware of the way her limbs ached, the way her skin was dry and peeling. The jellyfish welt on her arm was starting to scab and peel, and her hair had been jaggedly chopped off by the sword. It felt like there were burn marks on her shoulders, but she couldn't work out where they came from. She touched them carefully and felt huge, raised welts.

Everything hurt, but it wasn't just her limbs that felt bruised and battered. Something else was wrong, and whatever it was, it made her nervous. It wasn't until she'd emerged from the tunnels that she realized what it was: guilt. She felt bad—just a little bit—about last night. *Not that I should,* she told herself sternly. Cartwright was pompous and annoying, and anyway, she had to look out for herself. She forced the guilty feeling away, packing it tightly into a box in the back of her head.

"You were late," Scree said as she climbed the stairs from the catacombs into the house. "You can't get sloppy. Monsters have a bad temper."

"I know," she said bitterly.

"There's porridge for you in the kitchen," he added. "Not that you'll appreciate it. No one ever does."

He was looking at her disapprovingly, too, like he was waiting for her to say something. Then she remembered that her hair had been cut off.

"Well, thank you," she said, and gave him a look that said *don't even ask.*

"Meet me in the catacombs when you're done," he said. "You've got fishing to learn."

Realizing how hungry she was, Sophie crammed the porridge in her mouth like she'd never eaten before. She made a note to tell Scree how much she liked his cooking. Then she went into the darkness of the tunnels, drawn toward the old man's lantern like a peculiar moth. He was waiting at the bottom of a large slope, muttering and tapping his foot. When she drew near he began to walk, and the tunnels opened up before them, endless and whistling with the breath of the sea.

Sophie's foot hit something cold and spindly, and she yelped when she saw it was a huge, mechanical spider lying abandoned on the floor. They were everywhere, piled against the walls.

"Cleaning spiders," Scree said. "Laurel made 'em. You can wind one up if you want."

"No thanks."

Scree continued to weave his way through the tunnels as though guided by an invisible string, occasionally swinging his lantern toward the walls to chase away shadows.

"How far underground are we?" Sophie asked, trying not to sound worried.

"A long way," said Scree. "But we ain't drowning. We're going to the Glowfish Pits."

As soon as he said it the tunnel ended and they arrived

in a dim chamber the length of a swimming pool. The Glowfish Pits were holes bored deep into the ground like toothless gaps in an old mouth. There were hundreds of them, stretching from the front to the back of the chamber, making it look like the surface of a sponge. The water at the bottom of the pits was like crushed green glass, and in each one swam a group of sluggish, faintly luminous fish with lanterns above their heads.

"Glowfish," Scree said, balancing on one of the planks that stretched over the honeycomb floor. "Big one of these'll feed us for a week. Porridge, stew, roast, bake, pie, you name it, I can make it from glowfish. This is the only place they can live without the creatures getting 'em."

"Why are they glowing?" Sophie asked dubiously.

"They're haunted, aren't they," he said. "It's 'cause they live in the catacombs. There are ghosts down here, and ghosts like to haunt things that move, but they're simpleminded, don't realize they're just inhabiting fish." He snorted. "Don't move too slow or you'll get one, too."

"Where does the ghost go when you eat the fish?" she asked, testing her weight on a plank.

"They *dissipate*, don't they," he said. "Don't they teach you anything in school? That's why the windows are steamed up. Ghosts dissipatin'."

"Right," said Sophie. "We didn't really study ghosts at school. More oceanography and mathematics, that kind of thing."

"Go on, laugh," said Scree. "All the others did. You won't be smiling when you fall in 'cause you ain't been paying enough attention. The pits are deep."

"I won't fall in. I never get in tr—"

The plank she was standing on snapped in the middle. The last thing she saw was the back of Scree's head, and then she was falling, too surprised to scream or even take a breath. She hit the cold water far below. It slammed against her back like a solid wall. And then she was under the water, eyes wide open and staring into the face of a bloated, ghostly glowfish.

Her skirt puffed up like a life jacket, and she floated to the surface. The glowfish, which had fled when she landed, gathered back around her. Seemingly unperturbed by the new species in their water, they looked at her with the faces of morose, overweight humans.

"Has she run away?" she heard Scree mutter far above, somewhere beyond the circle of light. "Has she left poor old Scree to drag the catch back by himself?"

"I'm down here!" she shouted, but he'd gone conveniently deaf. "Mister Scree! I'm stuck!"

He sneezed and shuffled back. His face hovered over the hole.

"What are you doing?" he asked. Sophie tried to fling some water at him, but she only got it in her face.

"I fancied a swim," she said sarcastically.

"Bit cold down there," he observed.

"Do you think?" She tread water, waiting for him to say something else. "How do I get back up?"

"Beats me," he said, and disappeared.

"Hey!" she shouted, the words bouncing around the pit and scattering the glowfish again. "You can't just leave me here!"

She paddled awkwardly. The water was so deep she couldn't see the bottom, but there were definitely things down there that weren't glowfish; she could see them faintly pulsing and squirming, rising slowly upward like balloons.

She looked up at the sheer rock walls and tried to think of a way to climb back up, pretending that she wasn't extremely worried.

Scree returned, but instead of lowering a rope he slung a small waxed parcel down. She only just managed to grab it before it sank. Inside was a candle stub and a box of matches. *Excellent,* she thought. *Now I can see what's going to eat me.*

"Hold the candle up and look at the walls," said Scree. "I'll meet you at the other end."

"I—what?" His footsteps receded into the cavern and the light went with him, leaving her with nothing but the horrible luminescence. "The other end of what? I'm in a *hole*."

She managed to light the candle, and held it high above her head. For a minute she couldn't see a thing, then she realized that she was staring into a deep hole in the side of the pit. She swam to the other side, took a deep breath, and climbed through.

She landed in another network of tunnels and pits, smaller and more cramped than the catacombs above, and waist-deep in water. Glowfish swam around her as she held up the candle. She searched and saw, on the wall, a silvery arrow pointing toward another tunnel. The arrow had the same sickly look of the glowfish, like it had been painted with their blood, and it was only visible if she held the candle at a certain angle. She passed her hand in front of the light so the arrow flashed into and out of existence. Secret messages. She had to admire Scree's wiliness. She'd thought he had some kind of sixth sense in the dark, but he'd been following directions all along.

She waded through the tunnels, until she came to an

archway and a slope that went upward. Containing a whoop of delight, Sophie almost ran up it.

She emerged in a new chamber, and there was no water and no glowfish. The faintly glowing signs around the walls pointed to *the house* and *the pits*, and *emergency squid exit*, and . . . she squinted and moved closer to the wall.

"The Room of Remains," she muttered. There was a large *X* drawn next to it. Entry forbidden.

She heard footsteps echoing in the tunnel and quickly moved away from the sign. She wanted to see what the Room of Remains was, but she had the feeling Scree wouldn't be too happy with her if she poked her nose in. She continued up the slope and emerged somewhere close to the house, in a cavern filled with the murky light of the sea. She could hear the twins screaming upstairs, and the steady *drip, drip* of stalactites.

"I'm in here," she called to Scree, then noticed a hulking shape in the corner. Something huge was hidden under a moldering dust sheet. She went to it, wrinkling her nose at the pungent smell of mold.

The sheet fell to pieces under her touch. Beneath it was a machine, something made of metal which was now entirely green, a car-shaped thing with an engine of cogs and pistons. It had three arms on either side, each with a hinged elbow and a grab-claw hand. On the front was a bronze mask with a thin pipe emerging from its mouth. It wore a coat of thin, white mushrooms, and one of its arms was extended as though about to pour a cup of tea.

Sophie felt a jab in her shoulder. She dropped the candle, then felt embarrassed and scowled at Scree, who was lurking behind her.

"Didn't your parents ever tell you not to look at other people's things?" he barked.

"Lots," she said. She tried to stay annoyed, but the thing in front of her was too interesting. "What is it? Why has it got a face?"

"He thought it'd make it more approachable," said Scree.

The bronze mask had two streaks of rust running down from its eyes and from the corners of its mouth. It looked like it had been crying.

"Who did? And whoever it is, he was wrong."

"His lordship," said Scree. "Laurel, who built this house. Cartwright's uncle, the twins' father. You *know*. Neptune rest his soul an' give him lobsters in heaven. This is one of his inventions."

"It's sort of horrible."

"It makes coffee."

She tried to make sense of the pipes running through the thing's stomach, and gave up.

"It's big," she said. "Too big for a kitchen, even."

"That's why I put it down here," he said. "And to stop the twins from wrecking it. They ruined a lot of their father's stuff, and I don't want to see it all go to pieces. It ain't one of his best inventions, though. The inventions got worse, toward the end."

"Before he died?"

Scree winced. She touched the long front arm of the machine and ran her fingers down the joints, wondering why Laurel would give the machine such a sad expression.

"He made his best stuff right after he built the house, when the twins were young," said Scree. "The clock room with the bell, he made that for me. He made rooms that move around the house and machines that walk on two legs. Engines that collect oysters on their own, spiders that go up and dust the walls, lamps that light 'emselves. You'd swoon if you saw half the stuff he made." He sniffed. "Not that it's any of your business. I doubt you care."

"Why do the twins wreck his machines?" she asked. Despite herself, she did care a bit. Scree pressed his lips together, and for a moment she thought she'd asked too many questions. This was the most he'd ever spoken to her in one go.

"They're spirited," he said.

"No," she said carefully, looking sidelong at him. "They're maniacs. You don't have to be nice about them just because you're their servant. Why are you their servant, anyway? Do they actually pay you?"

"They're *spirited*," he repeated.

"They're psychotic."

"Don't you dare annoy 'em. You might think I'm a silly old man, but the only way to keep the peace in this house is to keep the twins happy. Not stir 'em up like Cartwright does."

Looking frustrated, he flicked the arm of the coffee machine, which sent a long, sonorous bell through the cavern.

"I didn't mean to upset you," said Sophie when it died away. Scree was looking at the machine as though it might explode. "I don't think you're silly. I think you're the only reason this place hasn't crumbled into the sea."

This made Scree cackle, long and loud. He patted the machine on the head, and for the first time he looked close to smiling.

"I'll tell you a secret," he said. "I'm not worried about

the twins, 'cause they're not bothered about me. I know what they really want."

"But they have everything they want! Including you running around after them, finding them pineapples. They love it."

"What they *want* is to grind Cartwright into the carpet," he said, tapping his nose. "When Cartwright turned up, Laurel really took to him. Taught him how to invent. The twins were jealous. Her Battleshipness was annoyed 'cause she wasn't leading the grand life she expected, so she encouraged all the smashing."

"Poor Laurel," she said.

"Aye. He was clever enough to change the world, but instead he got stuck here."

He stared at the hulking machine as though he could see the face of his dead master in there, and Sophie felt a twinge of sympathy. She wondered where Scree came from, whether he had a family somewhere, how he'd ended up on this horrible island. She thought Laurel might have been a good friend to him. She reached out and brushed some of the dirt off the face of the machine, and smiled at him.

"Anyway," he grumbled, "the *moral* is, don't talk to Cartwright."

"How's that the—"

"It just is."

"Right," she said.

"Good," he agreed. "I reckon we're done now. You should've brought some of the glowfish up with you. They're easy pickings down there. Easier than hauling 'em up on a line."

"I'll do better the next time I fall in," she said.

They left the cavern, Sophie following Scree through the gloomy tunnels, up and up toward the house. After a while he started to whistle a slow, summery tune that Sophie recognized from somewhere, the fairground perhaps. Then he broke off and turned to her craftily.

"There's time to pass before the next feeding," he said. "And you've wrung a story out of me, even if it wasn't fancy. What do I get in return?"

"What do you mean?"

"I heard you tell the boy a tale last night. Oh yes, I was there, hiding behind my mop. I want one, too."

"I don't have anything to tell you."

"You call yourself a storyteller?" he said, and snorted. "I thought you might be different, but you're just like all the other Bone Snatchers. Nothing to say for yourself."

"I've got plenty," she said.

"Go on, then."

She knew she was being tested, but for some reason she didn't mind. There was something about Scree that she was starting to like.

"All right," she said as they started walking again. "I was going to save it for a special occasion, but you've forced it out of me. I'll tell you the story of the skeleton fish."

Chapter 10

The Skeleton Fish

In Which We Find That Nobody Is Ever Really Dead

Hundreds of years before the sun and moon rose in a regular pattern, when the stars were newborn and the planet was a thin, fragile egg, there was a pit in the middle of the ocean. It was bottomless, and dark like a blanket, and teeming with young and frightened life.

There were countless fish in the pit, crammed together like tissues in a box: the bladderfish that emitted a putrid smell, the bookfish with its hundreds of white gills, the unfortunately named maggoty starfish, and thousands more, spiraling into the depths.

But the only truly remarkable fish were the skeleton fish, which had no visible flesh. There was nothing in or on them. They had empty eye sockets, and gaps between all their shining bones, and holes in their nonexistent hearts. They were deeply unhappy, in a special way that only fish can be.

But the sea provided for them. Many sailors drowned in storms, and refusing to cease existing, their ghosts attached themselves to the skeleton fish, giving them luminous flesh. Then the sailors' ghosts had bodies and the fish had a shape.

One day a girl with frosty hair dropped into the ocean, weighed down with a red stone, to find the crown of the sea. It had belonged to a drowned king who was now a glowfish. She took the crown and swam away.

The girl was triumphant but soon became deeply troubled; after all, she had stolen the crown from its rightful owner. Even if he was no longer a king, there had to be a way she could pay the glowfish back. And so, after swimming to the surface with the crown, she threw her prized red stone into the water. She had killed for that stone, and she missed it greatly, but it was more than a fair exchange. It made the king very happy, for it, unlike his crown, didn't remind him of being human, and it trapped the light and kept all the glowfish warm.

Even today, if someone dies on this island, their ghost will become a glowfish. And when the glowfish they inhabit dies, the ghost remembers the kind gift of the red stone and keeps watch over those that live on their island. They attach them-

selves to all the water drops in the house, growing into colonies of mold and beautiful umbrella-like mushrooms. They make the house see and hear and breathe. They do this so the people inside know they will never be alone, and that their dead will never be truly lost.

Chapter 11

The Room of Remains

Sophie spent the rest of the day collecting bones and trying to avoid Cartwright. As she plucked skeleton bits from the ground, trying not to look, her mind went to all the places that she did not want it to.

She kept thinking about last night, when she'd tried to escape, and couldn't shut away the feeling that she had been wrong.

Her parents had always called her selfish and bad-blooded, bent on getting her own way just to torture them. She'd gone to their stupid parties, and worn their horrible clothes, and smiled and told all her parents' friends how wonderful school was, but she lied through her teeth the whole time. In the end it had always gone wrong, and she ended up bursting and telling people what she really thought and embarrassing everyone, and feeling secretly glad about it. But now she wondered if her parents were right about her all along.

She was angry at herself for being so self-centered and almost dooming Cartwright. She was angry at herself for not being more apologetic to him. She was angry that she didn't even *feel* like being more apologetic to him.

Selfish, selfish, selfish!

No wonder her parents had run away without her. Maybe on the New Continent they'd have another child, and this one would be nice. And Sophie would be stuck here forever, left with nothing but the sea and a lingering sense of doom.

She threw the sack down and strode around, then came back because she needed the bones to feed the sea creatures. Today they were playful and flicked water at her, but she wasn't in the mood to forgive them for last night's attack.

All day she paced, ducking when she heard the twins' footsteps or Scree's creaky knees. She stood by a window and spent an hour watching the place where the tidal path used to be.

Night fell, and the sea pounded the island in a frenzy. Sophie stayed awake, dreading a sudden wave or the caves collapsing. Water dripped through the ceiling, forming a puddle by her head, so that every time she turned over she got a mouthful of brine.

When the storm was over the house began to settle, creaking and complaining in the dark. The catacombs breathed in, pulling damp air into the island's lungs. Still she couldn't sleep. Her hair skittered and slid toward the tunnels like she was being sucked in.

Like a sleepwalker, Sophie got up and walked into the catacombs.

In the blackness she took a candle from her pocket. She didn't remember putting it there, nor the matches that her fingers groped for and struck. The death mask of the hulking coffee machine beast flared up in front of her. The shadows of its beverage-making arms criss-crossed on the walls, forming a cage. It now appeared to be grinning.

The face startled her, and her fingers loosened so the candle slipped through and extinguished. She bent down and grabbed it, matches scattering from her pockets. She was alone in the dark.

Even while her skin crawled at the thought of going any farther, Sophie knew that she had come here for a reason. Her mind was churning, and the only way she could distract herself was by searching the guts of this awful, weird house, which nagged her like an itch. Maybe then she would think of a way to escape it.

As she was deciding where to go, the machine behind her moved. It groaned quietly, like it might just be settling, but then the noise grew and grew, like the machine's arms were straining, and just as Sophie was about to flee it settled with a loud *clonk*. She swept her hands over the floor until she found one of the matches, lit the candle, and swinging it into the face of the beast found it exactly where it had been.

She knew the noise must have been the wind, but the machine looked like a bug waiting to open its shell and scuttle forward. Her hands were shaking, but she gritted her teeth and moved quickly, sweeping the walls with her candle to look for the glowfish arrows, retracing the path she'd taken during the day. After an eternity of stumbling she emerged in the chamber of signs.

There were directions and messages scrawled everywhere in glowing paint. The wall was dominated by a bad drawing of a squid with each of its tentacles pointing in a different direction: *House. Potato garden. Sewer.* And there was the sign from before: *The Room of Remains*, with a line trailing away from the last letter and snaking through a gap in the wall. The remains of what? Bodies? Inventions? Or was it a giant rubbish dump?

Casting one last look behind her, fighting the strange feeling that the coffee machine might have trundled down after her, she squeezed through the gap in the wall and began to walk.

The sounds of the house died behind her. The silvery line faded into a scratch that tripped and jolted over the wall, breaking and reappearing like an unsteady heartbeat. Shuddering, Sophie passed a green waterfall that fed a rotting pond and tripped over an abandoned glove that looked like a dismembered hand. The ceiling dropped until she had to bend over, then kept dropping until she was on her hands and knees, gravel scraping across her legs. For the first time ever Sophie felt claustrophobic. She could suffocate down here; if anything collapsed there wouldn't be time to get out.

She crawled around a bend and came up against a slab of rock. The dead end was a tiny stub of space, and the silvery arrow ended in a spatter, like its painter had run into the wall.

There was no room to turn around, so to get out she'd have to crawl backward the way she came. Frustrated, she started shuffling back, moving inch by inch on her hands and knees until with a perfectly timed sputter the candle went out.

"Come on," she muttered desperately. All her matches were scattered on the floor of the cave farther back. With the darkness cramming in on her, the dead end felt like a coffin. There was a low, mechanical groan from somewhere far behind her, and the sound of—what? Wheels? *Nonsense. It's the house settling again.* But it really did sound like the scraping of wheels. A pained screech, like grinding metal. Someone was behind her. Or something.

A wet drop landed on her head, and for a moment she thought *blood,* and her whole body went cold. She looked up and saw a crack of light far above. Water was slowly trickling down from it. The dead end was a chimney.

Sophie had never given much thought to the god of the sea before, but she immediately promised that she'd sacrifice as many mussels as he could eat if he got her out in one piece. Abandoning the candle, she felt the wall. If she sucked her stomach in, she could just about stand up. Something clattered at the other end of the tunnel, the sound ricocheting around its curves like a bullet. Cutting off a yelp, she began to climb.

Her damp hands kept slipping, and she couldn't bend her knees properly without getting stuck between the two walls. The chimney was tall, and she was certain that if she fell she would break her neck.

Her hands finally met a ledge at the top. She could see the crack properly now, but that's all it was: a hairline fracture of light. She pushed her fingers against it, hoping she could break the rock away.

Her hand went through the ceiling like she'd plunged it into cake mix. The top of the chimney had been covered by nothing more than decaying carpet. She took a deep breath, felt for the edge of the hole, and grabbed it with both hands so she was swinging. She pulled herself up, legs pedaling the air, and wriggled through the hidden gap at the top of the cave.

Her head pushed aside the dark swathe of carpet. She emerged in a corridor in the house, right beneath a grand, rotting table with the world's most hideous mermaid-shaped vase on top, which fell off and landed in front of her nose with a damp *thud* that made her shudder. Both ends of the corridor were boarded up, although at one end the planks were split, as though someone had recently forced their way in.

It didn't look like anybody had lived in this part of the house for a while. The wallpaper sustained huge colonies of exotic-colored molds. There was a portrait of Laurel and the twins, a bit like the one she had seen before, except the man's face had been scrawled on with black paint.

In front of her was a locked door, and pinned to it was a damp piece of paper: *NO ENTRY. WE MEAN IT.*

She placed the mermaid vase on the table and looked through the keyhole.

She was met by a skeletal dinosaur on wires with its jaw hanging open, swooping toward her like it was about to snap the door handle off. Behind it there were stacks of crates with jars of starfish balanced on top. There were complex cabinets, a steam-powered wooden horse, books, and stacks of paper. There was half a piano and a gramophone with three horns. These must have been Laurel's inventions.

Whoever had collected this stuff was either a compulsive hoarder or looking for something. Sophie had the distinct impression that all this junk has been combed through, pulled apart, and shoved back together in the wrong order.

I'm going in, she told herself. In the pause that followed, she swore she could hear the machine again. It felt like the house had turned to listen. There was a long, low creak, and something scraped across the floor at the other end of the corridor. She put her hands over her ears, but she could hear her pulse and the rush of her own blood, which was worse.

Don't stop to think. Just go!

The door was locked, but that had never stopped her before, and she was good at breaking things. She only needed to kick the lock twice before the door around it splintered, and even though her shoes were as thin as paper she barely felt the impact.

She shouldered her way through the door to stand in the middle of the chaos.

She could see now how the dinosaur had been smashed to pieces and reassembled in the most unlikely way, its rib bones protruding through its eye sockets, its great spine twisted like a paper clip. There were toys that looked like they belonged in an asylum, dolls with legs for arms and a yellow crane with metal spider legs, a train with its insides gutted. And then there were machines. Tiny things with brass levers, and huge, hulking contraptions that looked like they could be used to move elephants. A slew of cogs lays across the floor as though thrown in a temper. The Room of Remains, indeed.

Far away a door slammed shut and Sophie froze, panic beating against her chest like a trapped bird, but a minute later nobody came and she breathed out again. *My name is Sophie Seacove*, she told herself, trying to calm down. *I am good at telling stories. I'm immune to Sea Fever, and I'm having an adventure.*

As she stepped forward sheets of paper crackled under her feet. She looked down at a sea of blotched and hurried notes, pictures of skeletons and monsters. There was a close-up of a sea monster's ear, gnarled and explosively shaped like a cauliflower, and then another, and another. There were hundreds of pictures of ears. Each was exquisitely detailed, the lines so fine they must have been done under a microscope. Whoever drew these was very good. And very obsessed.

She glanced over her shoulder, then bent down and read some of the notes scribbled in the margins of a diagram.

Tear it down burn it down.

J'fish did a dance in response to B'hoven was it the pitch or does it like it?

Are they stupid? I was trying to help.

He can never find out, poor boy.

HELP ME!

And, curling from the ear of a particularly ugly squid: *My sandwich was moldy again. Scree says he made it for me weeks ago.*

Did the diagrams belong to Laurel? If these were his notes, then it sounded like he was very worried about something.

As Sophie turned away, a red box caught her eye. She flicked the catch to see what was inside.

The lid burst open and hit the wall so hard the hinges broke, and a huge clown, torso attached to a thick spring, fell forward. Heart hammering, Sophie picked the clown up, sweeping the red hair away from its face.

It was Cartwright in every way, from its high cheekbones to its staring eyes and the slight curl of a smile. It would have been a normal toy once, but someone had skillfully mutilated it. She shuddered as it bobbed backward and forward.

She pressed the clown back into the box and forced the lid down. She wanted to get out and pretend she was never in here.

A red light flickered in the corridor. Sophie spun around, knees catching the splinters in the floorboards.

"Poke, poke," someone whispered.

She wasn't alone.

She slid backward until she was pressed against a cabinet. She could hear her own body like a factory, bones creaking, eyelids closing and clicking open again. Every inch of movement was a cacophony of noise.

The voice was hushed by another, and they both giggled. Her fear was replaced by a wrench of disgust. The twins.

"I know it's you," she said. "What do you want?"

"The question is," said Ralf's voice, suddenly very close by, "what do *you* want? We know why you're up here. We know what you're after. But you won't find it. It's ours."

"What's yours?" she said as she started to tiptoe toward the door, crawling her hand toward a pair of silver scissors that were abandoned on a dresser.

"We're not stupid," said the invisible Ralf. "You want the Monster Box. Cartwright has sent you to look for it, hasn't he? You're not the first. You won't be the last, either. Now get out of our room and get away from our house, before we drive you into the sea."

"You're not driving me anywhere," she said, then grabbed the scissors and ran into the corridor. It was empty, but the door that had been boarded up was now hanging open like a hungry mouth. Red light flickered in the room beyond it. Footsteps pounded away, followed by a noise like a stone being rolled over a tomb. Silence again.

"Do you want me to follow you?" she said, holding the scissors out in front of her. No answer. "Is this a game?"

Still nothing. She looked back to the room full of junk. Then at the false floor under the table, imagining the long, slippery climb down.

She walked toward the light.

Chapter 12

The Red Rabbit Run

The walls on the other side of the broken door were bathed in red. There were red lanterns on the ceiling and red candles attached to the walls on long bronze arms. The carpet was red and streaked with deep grooves like someone had been dragged across it.

Hidden somewhere far in front of her in the twisting, cramped corridor, Sophie heard one of the twins whistle a lazy tune.

"I get it," said Sophie, treading toward the sound like she was approaching a wild animal. "You're trying to scare me away. What are you so afraid of me finding?"

The whistling continued.

"You said something about a box," she said, tightening her grip on the scissors. "First I've heard of it. But I'm interested now. There must be something awfully good inside it, if Cartwright wants it, too."

The whistling stopped. So did she, standing in the middle of the red corridor. There was no sound. Nothing moved.

"When I see you, I won't think twice about using these," she said, holding the scissors blade-out, throwing her voice into the emptiness. When there was no reply her anger rose like a tentacle emerging from the sea. "Tell me what you want or stop messing around!"

The sound of scraping furniture, two people giggling. There were gaps inside the walls, Sophie realized, and the twins were sliding through them like termites. It was all theater tricks—the red light, the secret passages, that stupid whistling—but somehow she couldn't make it feel like make-believe. She gritted her teeth and walked down the corridor, through patches of black and into pools of red light. Black, red. Black, red. She couldn't see more than three feet in front of her.

The footsteps started again, *thud-thud-thud*, as the twins bolted through the pools of darkness in front of her. For a second she saw their shadows, stretched thin with hands raised like claws. She stuck the scissors in her pocket and ran after them.

She rounded a corner and emerged in another wonderland of junk. It rose on either side of her, forming a maze built of salvaged treasure. Sophie entered the maze, which stretched across the whole room, and turned left, left, left again. She fought through cramped gangways, hands raised to grab one of the twins should they dart in front of her.

"You won't catch us, Silverfish," said the voice of Ralf, or at least she thought it was Ralf. He appeared on top of a stack of furniture, the flickering light throwing red shadows over his face. "But don't worry. We won't hurt you too much."

"You can't hurt me," she said, but she found that her hand was on the scissors. "You're overgrown children."

"We're very mature for our age," said Ralf. Gail grew out of the shadows beside him, crouching on top of a cupboard. "Besides, we're older than you. And I'm an hour older than Gail, of course."

"Ten minutes," corrected Gail, and he echoed his brother's smile.

Sophie slid around the corner of a stack. Ralf swiveled to watch her.

"Why are you doing this?" she asked. Her eyes slid around the mess, looking for a way out. "Are you teaching me a lesson?"

The twins both rose, their shadows growing like monsters

behind them. Sophie pressed herself against a tower of books, trying to work out how she could push them and run.

"You shouldn't stick your nose in where it doesn't belong," said Ralf. He strolled over the top of the maze, stepping neatly from stack to stack. Sophie scrambled away as he passed over her head.

"This is our house," said Gail. "Our stuff. And nobody can take it away from us, not even Cartwright."

"All of this is because you're jealous of your cousin?" said Sophie. "You're pathetic. He's not trying to take anything away from you."

"He is!" hissed Ralf, and swung down suddenly so his face was upside down in front of hers, stretched like a mask. "He wants our box! Just because our father gave it to him, it doesn't mean it's *his*."

Sophie fled through the stacks of books and found herself blocked off by Gail.

"It's ours by right," said Gail. "*He* can't have it. He'd ruin everything."

"I have no idea what you're talking about!" she yelled. She wrenched a book from the pile and threw it at Gail's head. He ducked neatly and the book vanished in a cloud of dust behind him.

"Don't lie to us," said Ralf behind her. "You don't want

to know what happened the last time a servant made us angry. It was very messy."

Sophie took off again, and the twins cackled delightedly, but they weren't following her anymore. Within minutes she had fought her way through the maze to the door at the other end of the room. Sophie knew that something was very wrong, that she got away too easily, but she was already pushing the door open. She could feel the weight of something above it and ducked, but not quickly enough.

The contents of the bucket hit her with a visceral slap, and she was drenched in thick, nose-burning paint. It was old and sticky and—she looked at her hands, and nearly shouted with horror—it was crimson, bloody. She tried to get it out of her eyes, which were sticking together, as she ran into the next corridor.

"Go on, Silverfish," sang Ralf. "Try and get away. We know this place like our own faces."

"That's enough!" she screamed, but she was running, and there were doors slamming behind her, more laughter, and those incessant footsteps. She rattled the handle of one of the doors, but it was locked. The twins knew she was going to come down here, just like they knew she would end up exploring the house and coming across the

Room of Remains. They'd been herding her through it like she was in a rabbit run, and she'd been stupid enough to fall for it. She hurtled down the corridor, burning with fury and horror, dripping what looked like blood but felt like syrup, trying each door and finding them all locked, until finally one swung open.

The twins had grown quiet now. Only their footsteps *tap-tap-tapped* toward her. For a second, Sophie hesitated outside the room. Then she slammed the door shut again and continued down the corridor, leaving the room empty, squeezing herself against the wall and praying that she was invisible.

She heard Ralf and Gail stop outside the door. They whispered something to each other and giggled.

"We know you're in there, Silverfish," said Ralf to the empty room. "There's no way out but through the window, and nothing underneath but the sea and our wriggly, ravenous, carnivorous friends. Can you see them? Are you scared?"

"How long shall we make her stay in there?" Gail whispered. "Shall we make the monsters angry, so they try and come through the window?"

Sophie continued to creep down the corridor and, reaching a dead end, opened a cupboard and slipped inside.

A dim yellow light flickered on, humming gently. The first thing she saw was her own face a hundred times over. She reached out with a hand, and the other Sophies reached out to her, until their fingertips met coldly on the mirror. Four of them, one on every side, covered in paint, bouncing her back into infinity. She almost laughed when she realized that the paint wasn't red at all, but white. It was only the light that had made it seem that way.

She could see her back, her torn and ragged clothes, and for the first time, the marks on her skin.

She pulled down the shoulder of her dress and saw the row of circles across her back, dwindling in size until they reached a point on her shoulder blade. Purple, perfectly neat, raised like brand marks. She was covered in the scars from the squid that peeled her off the rock the other day. And her jagged hair, her hollow cheeks, the bruises all over her body—she looked insane. Dangerous.

She kind of liked it.

There was a row of brass buttons on the cupboard wall, the inscriptions next to them faded into obscurity. She ran her fingers over them but couldn't make out anything except, maybe, numbers.

Farther up the corridor, Ralf knocked on the door of the room.

"Silverfish?" he said. "Why are you ignoring us?" She heard the door creak open. "Silverfish?"

Through the crack in the cupboard doors she saw Gail turn and look straight at her. Without thinking, she jabbed one of the buttons on the wall. The twins shouted furiously and pounded toward her, and she hit her fist against the whole control panel as they loomed out of the dark.

The cupboard jerked like it'd been shot awake, and Sophie fell against one of the mirrors. There was a *click* as the doors locked themselves together, and the twins fell against the other side of them, howling. Then it felt like she was falling, her stomach plunging into her mouth, the whirr of invisible machinery shaking her skull, the sound of the twins flying away like they'd been dragged off by a malevolent spirit. This time, Sophie did scream. Words appeared before her as the light sputtered:

WELCOME TO LAUREL'S PATENT LIFTING ROOM!

The bottom of the cupboard hit something and bounced. Sophie dropped to the floor. The doors clicked open. And then, just like that, she was facing the oyster beach, just inside the mouth of the catacombs where she usually emerged to feed the creatures. Without a backward look she flew out of the cupboard, which whirred and took off again.

She staggered away and onto the beach, gasping in the fresh air. Her legs were uncontrollable with the shock of flying.

She staggered to a halt beside a rock pool and looked back. Hysteria bubbled up her throat and she bent over, clutching herself, laughing maniacally like one of the twins. She was safe. There was nothing to be scared of. She looked up at the trail of footprints she'd left, glowing like a path back to the catacombs.

With a last hiccup she peeled her shoes and socks off, storing the scissors carefully inside them—just in case— and wriggled her toes in the cool water. The twins were somewhere upstairs, shouting at each other, their voices drifting through a smashed window, then fading as they retreated. She stepped into the rock pool and waded in up to her knees, and the paint bled from her skin, turning the water cloudy. She sluiced water over her shoulders, then lay down so she was floating faceup, her skirt billowing out from her with trapped air.

She stayed there for a long time, until her whole body felt numb with the cold and the moon was printed on her eyelids. She wondered what her parents were doing now.

Were they sucking the meat off a huge lobster or drinking cocktails in the shallows of a warm pool? Were they wondering what *she* was doing now? Whatever they imagined, it couldn't be this.

Something touched her toes. She withdrew her foot quickly, then sat and watched as an octopus with a head no larger than an egg undulated over her skin. It wrapped its tentacles around her foot and began to squeeze, making her toes click like they were popping out of their sockets. She tried to pry it off, but the harder she pulled the tighter it stuck, until it felt like all the blood was leaving her foot.

"Stop it," she said hopelessly. "I've just escaped a pair of psychotic morons. I'm not going to be hurt by a—ow!"

It suckered itself to her whole foot with a *pop*.

"I'm being attacked by a very small octopus in a rock pool," she said to herself. The creature wound a tentacle around her sixth toe, prodding it and flattening its body to her skin as though it were trying to hug her. It gently waved a tentacle toward the sea.

Suddenly, she understood what she was meant to do. She scrambled out of the pool and, hopping awkwardly on one foot, went down to the sea and put her foot in. The octopus released itself with a cloud of ink. Before it left it spread its bluish tentacles and wound them around her toes again, weaving from her big toe to her tiny sixth one, as though counting, then, satisfied, shot off in a cloud of bubbles.

"See you later," Sophie said, and the sea whispered back its approval, touching her ankles like an old friend.

Chapter 13

Breakfast Time

"Avast!"

It wasn't the feeding bell that woke Sophie but the Battleship's cry, echoing along the tunnels and going through her head like a drill. She fell out of bed, where she'd gone to sleep soaking wet, and started pulling on her shoes and coat before she'd properly woken up. She was halfway out of the tunnels before she heard the cry again.

"Avast! Avast!"

She ran onto the oyster beach, shoelaces flapping, to see the Battleship struggling with something in the water. Up to her knees in the waves, the huge woman was having a tug-of-war with a sea creature, heaving on the end of a long, white rope. She was clearly losing. Sophie hit the water and tried to pull her away, but it was like shouldering an iceberg.

"It's going to pull you under," she panted. "It's bigger than you!"

"It won't win," the woman growled, and grinding her teeth heaved on the rope again. It started to rip loudly, and Sophie realized that it wasn't a rope after all: the monster had the Battleship's twisted, stretched petticoat in its mouth. It finally broke, the Battleship fell back, and the creature howled triumphantly. It snapped up the petticoat and dove under the water, releasing an odor of rotten eggs.

"What are you doing out here?" Sophie asked. "How did it get your petticoat?"

"I couldn't sleep," the Battleship said shortly, her skirt wallowing around her. She didn't make an effort to get up. "I wanted to see the monsters. They used to listen to me. They respected me."

"I don't think they respect anyone," Sophie replied.

"Ha! You would say that. You're young. They like young girls. They have softness for them, you'll see. But it's gone for me now. Everything's gone for me."

"I wouldn't worry about it," said Sophie, though she had no idea what the Battleship was talking about.

"You don't know. I haven't slept well in years. My bed is a funny shape. It feels like I'm sleeping on a bomb."

The Battleship got up, water pouring off her like a beach ball.

"Breakfast," she said. "It's time. You may join us if you wish."

With that she glided off, the back of her ruined skirt rustling. Sophie turned toward the sea, where the creature was eyeing her hungrily with a piece of petticoat between its teeth. She stomped into the water and kicked a stone at it.

"You shouldn't do that," she told it. "I know you can't understand me, but I'm telling you anyway. And that was your breakfast, by the way. I'm not feeding you again."

A flat-headed octopus the size of a horse lunged from the water. It sucked the bottom of Sophie's coat into its mouth, which was full of teeth as small and brown as apple seeds. Sophie was spun around and pulled backward, but she regained her balance just in time and pulled back as hard as she could.

"I said NO!" she shouted, and to her surprise it let go and shot back into the water. She gathered her coat around her and stormed back to the catacombs, surrounded by the bubbling, inhuman laughter of the creatures. There was a large hole in her coat, and the bottom half of her skirt was missing, too.

"You didn't win," she called over the water. "I wanted a change anyway."

Ten minutes later Sophie kicked through the doors of a wardrobe that had been glued shut with grime and barnacles. Everything else in the abandoned bedroom had fallen to pieces, but the wardrobe was like a time capsule, perfectly sealed and dry. It was the fifth one she'd tried that morning. And unlike the others, this one contained exactly what she needed.

She took a pair of black trousers, a shirt, a pair of boots, and a frock coat. Looking in the mirror, she thought she looked like a pirate. Yes, this outfit was much better than her foul old dress. She threw it out the window toward the sea, and for good measure tossed her old shoes out, too.

"I changed my mind," she called out the window. "You get seconds!"

She slammed the window as the water began to seethe and the monsters started fighting over the scraps.

Sophie marched down to the dining room, where breakfast was being served by Scree. She could hear the twins inside, gobbling their food and slurping their tea, and the entirely one-sided conversation Cartwright was trying to politely have with his aunt. She took a deep breath. There would be no more hiding from Cartwright or the twins.

She threw the doors open. The sun was streaming in, and dust motes pirouetted around her. From the windows, the sea glittered like something from the poster of the New Continent. This tiny moment threw her. When she looked back she saw the twins, their faces blank and polite, and Gail pushed a plate of toast over to her.

"Hello," he said. "Are you hungry?"

Ralf picked up a slab of butter, which he licked like it was ice cream. He wiped his mouth with the back of his hand and said, "Sit."

"I don't want to," Sophie said.

She thought they were going to argue with her, but Gail only shrugged and crammed the toast into his mouth. She stared at them, looking for a blob of paint, a hint of embarrassment, a single glint of triumph in their faces. Cartwright pulled out the chair next to him.

"Scree made scrambled glowfish," he said. "It's . . . unusual."

Sophie stared at the twins again, willing them to say

something incriminating. Their hands were completely clean of paint. She looked at her own nails, which she'd scrubbed clean last night. She did scrub them, didn't she? Or was she imagining things? She sat down and gingerly picked up a fork as the Battleship swept half a kipper into her mouth.

"There's paint on your shoulder," she said to Ralf.

"There's not," he said without looking.

"And on your face," she said, and they stared at each other for a few seconds. Ralf didn't even blink.

Scree came in, dragging a trolley piled with plates of green jelly.

"Wasn't expecting extra people," he said, wrinkling his nose at Sophie. "Ain't enough jelly for you, too. You could have mine, I suppose. It doesn't matter. I can go hungry. I'll just have yesterday's fish. Never mind old Scree."

"You enjoy your jelly," she said to him as Ralf poked his with a long finger and the Battleship inhaled hers. Scree gave her a sour look and shuffled off again. Sophie realized with a pang of guilt that he must have cleaned up the paint-splattered mess that she trailed all through the house.

"What on earth happened last night?" Cartwright murmured as the twins tried to build their jelly into castles.

"They haven't thrown a single thing at me this morning. They're *pleased* with themselves."

"I'm not sure," she said, then remembered that she was annoyed with him. "You're not meant to be talking to me, are you? I'm the Great Betrayer."

"I've forgiven you," he said.

"How kind."

"I've forgiven you for stealing my clothes, too," he said. "They suit you."

"You shouldn't leave your things lying around in old wardrobes," she said, suddenly irritable. "Why have you forgiven me? What's in it for you?"

"Everything," he said. "Shall we at least be polite to each other? I think it could be mutually beneficial."

"What are you two driveling on about?" asked Ralf dangerously, flicking a lump of jelly toward them.

"Your wonderful nails," said Cartwright. "Do you file them into points, or are they natural?"

"You're a creep, Cartwright."

"You're a blithering little idiot."

"Your face looks like it was hit with a really boring spade."

"I'm sorry about your face. It must be terribly hard for you."

"Shut up!" barked the Battleship, bringing her fist

down on her plate, which cracked in half. "I'm sick of your bickering."

"Yes. Do something fun or we'll scream," said Gail, fingers twitching impatiently.

"Let's have a play!" shouted Ralf, leaping out of his seat.

"Great," said Cartwright.

The twins jumped onto the table, kicking all of the dishes and cutlery out of the way. They sang completely out of time with each other, stamping their feet so the table shook. Their eyes were fixed on Sophie and Cartwright, and she knew it was a ploy to stop them talking, but they soon got carried away and started dancing up and down, slipping through the jelly and snorting with laughter when they landed on their backs. The Battleship picked up her butter knife as though contemplating a murder.

Sophie grabbed hold of Cartwright and pulled him under the table.

The thick tablecloth muffled the sound of falling cutlery, but the air vibrated with the twin's stamping and horrible laughter.

"I know what you want from me," Sophie said. "You want something called the Monster Box. I don't know what's in it, but you're going to ask me to find it for you, and in return you'll get me to the New Continent. That's right, isn't it?"

He stared at her, so she continued: "I'm not stupid. The twins are already trying to stop me."

"I underestimated you," he said. "You're quite sharp."

"As Ralf's nails," she said. "Tell me what's in the box or I won't do it."

The noise above them stopped. They both held their breath.

"Applause! Applause!" shouted Gail, and Scree, who had secreted himself in a corner somewhere, clapped weakly.

"Well done, young sirs . . ."

"Don't clap, Scree," said the Battleship, and he stopped.

"Clap!" said Ralf.

"Don't you dare!"

"ANOTHER ONE!" shouted Gail, and they started again, cheering themselves as they stamped across the table.

"I don't know *exactly* what's in the box," Cartwright said. "I never had a chance to find out."

"You're telling me that you came all the way here for a box that your mad old uncle gave you, and you don't even know what it's for? Let them have it!"

"It's important," he said.

"Do you know that for a fact, or is it just a feeling?"

"You help me and I'll help you. I can't do it myself, not with both of them hounding me at once. If we work together we're as strong as they are."

"Is this box worth all the trouble?"

"If my suspicions are correct, it will save the world," he said.

The twins' song finished, and Scree clapped again. They jumped around on the table, whooping and applauding themselves.

"Hey, where did Silverfish and Cartwright go?" said Gail.

"You're ridiculous," said Sophie. "And you're mad. I don't trust you."

He beamed. "Meet me in the courtyard this afternoon. And be careful of the twins."

Sophie glared at him. The twins whipped the tablecloth away and light flooded in. Their heads appeared, upside down.

"Camping," said Gail. "Can we play?"

Sophie crawled out from under the table. Ralf dropped jelly on her head.

"Whoops," he said.

She scraped it out and flung it right back.

"Whoops," she said. She scrambled up and sat at the table again, among all the wreckage. She slid her hand into her pocket and felt the silver scissors that she'd stolen last night, and which she'd kept, just in case. She was having an idea.

"How about a story?" she said. "A good one. If I tell you a story, will you let everyone eat breakfast in peace?"

The twins considered the offer. It was possible to see the corners of their lips twitching as they tried to work out what the catch was. Gail was the first to give in.

"Let's hear it, then," he said. "I bet it's rubbish."

"I bet it's not," said Sophie.

"Does it have blood in it?" said Ralf.

"It begins," said Sophie, looking at them all, "with a murder."

Chapter 14

The Tailor

In Which We Learn Why Scissors Are Dangerous

On the windswept coast of a gray land there was a tall and terrible scissor factory. It was made of steel, and it had doors that could withstand an army. Every day hundreds of workers filed in and out, walking in unison because the steady snip, snip *of the scissor-making machines was drummed into their hearts.*

The scissor factory was run by the Tailor. While the scissor-making machines ran, he sat in his tower designing the newest pair of blades. He created scissors that were huge and silver, small and gold, stone and shell, scissors you could eat, and scissors with curved blades that looked like a parrot's beak.

"I like scissors," interrupted Gail, and everyone looked at him. It felt like someone had punched a hole in the glass between them and Sophie. She blinked, confused.

"Shut up," said Ralf.

"Yes, shut up," said Cartwright. "Both of you."

"The Tailor liked scissors, too," said Sophie, and their heads swiveled back. She grasped blindly for the tail end of the story. "That's why nobody liked him."

He loved the way their long blades went snip, snip. *Each pair he made was beautiful and satisfying in a way nobody could put their finger on (and wouldn't want to put their finger in between, because each pair was sharp as a razor clam). When a new design was brought out, people would line up in front of their local scissor shop to get their hands on the first pair.*

But one night one of the workers, a blade inspector, crept into the factory to steal the Tailor's latest designs. He was caught by the pearl polisher, who was still working, and a fight ensued. In the morning the pearl polisher was found dead with a pair of Silver Snips in his heart. The murderer had fled, and it was the Tailor who discovered the body. The factory workers saw the Tailor standing over the pearl polisher, and each, seizing a pair of scissors, chased the Tailor from the factory and into the sea.

As was his habit, the Tailor had his favorite pair of scissors up his sleeve. They were long and keen, and as he entered the water, the chopping of a hundred pairs of scissors behind him, he drew them out and opened the blades.

The workers thought he was trapped. There were sea creatures in the water, huge and hungry ones that ate whoever went near them. But the Tailor slipped and slid across the tidal path, toward an island so full of holes it was like a peach stone, and every time a creature came near him—snip! snip!—he cut off their tentacles.

He lived on the island for the rest of his life, with nothing to eat but the roaming tentacles he chopped off for his dinner, and nothing to drink but the salt water which eventually made him mad. He could never return to the mainland, because day and night there was someone waiting on the beach with a pair of his scissors. Eventually, after eating a poison-tipped squid, he died.

"Right," said Ralf. "I knew that was going to happen."

Sophie's head jerked up and the vision cleared again. Both the twins were trailing their fingers through the slime on the table, although Cartwright and the Battleship were staring at her like they'd seen her have a fit.

"You didn't know what was going to happen," said Sophie. "Anyway, that's cheating."

"We did a play like it once," said Gail. "I was the pair of scissors."

"I like it," interrupted the Battleship, shifting forward on her throne. "I feel sorry for the Tailor. He must have felt very alone."

"Oh, stop making it about you," said Ralf. "We know *you* feel alone. You married father for his oysters. It's your own fault you don't have anything left."

"This house," she said, "is mine."

"This house is ours. We just let you stay here because you're too heavy to move."

The Battleship looked at them with barely suppressed rage. Cartwright put his hand over his aunt's and said, "Don't listen to them."

Sophie had assumed that Cartwright hated his aunt, but even she felt some pity for the woman, who looked sad and deflated.

"Oh, listen to Cartwright sucking up," Ralf said with a sneer. "She does it for attention. Next she'll start whining about how bad she feels about driving our father insane."

"I rather think *you* drove him insane," said Cartwright.

"Besides, Mother," said Ralf, "you must remember that we're on the same side. We're both trying to protect the same thing, aren't we?"

From the corner of her eye Sophie saw Cartwright's free hand tighten around his spoon. The Battleship pulled her hand away from his and pushed the table aside so she could get out. She swooped over to the door, and Ralf cackled, long and loud.

"I'm going to get you one day," Cartwright warned Ralf. "It's your fault my uncle went mad. I'm going to grab you by your scrawny little neck and—"

"He returned!" shouted Sophie. Everyone stopped and looked at her. Ralf's mouth began to open, so she plowed on before he could make any more noise. "The Tailor. He came back."

"Oh, yeah?" said Gail.

"Yeah. He rose from the dead."

Cartwright looked at her murderously, but he let go of the spoon. Sophie thought again about the scissors, and a plan began to form. She didn't know how or when she would use it. But it was there, uncurling like a streamer, along with the wicked urge to teach them all a lesson.

"The Tailor rose from the dead," she said calmly.

***

His death should have been the end of him, but he was full of hate for his factory workers, and hate is one of the only things strong enough to drag a dead man back to his own body. He rose from his resting place looking for revenge.

The island he haunted became Catacomb Hill, and his ghost is still here. At night he wanders the house with his scissors, and every time he turns a corner they go snip, snip. *If you hear that sound you'd better run. When he sees someone he doesn't like the look of, he leaps on to their back and stabs them with his pair of scissors.*

Legend has it that if you catch the ghost, you will be granted three and a half wishes by the Tailor. Power, fame, immortality—you could have anything.

The chance comes once in a lifetime, but what a lifetime it would be. You would rule the world.

Chapter 15

Scree's Warning

Sophie had created something monstrous with her story. All day she fought the sensation that a character had crept out of it and was following her around. Everywhere she went there was rustling behind her, creaking floors, and shadows that flickered just a second after she passed. Either the Tailor's ghost had oozed out of the walls, or she was being followed by a sea creature that had learned to quietly walk on the tips of its tentacles. It wasn't a crazy idea. It happened on her street last year, when the local constable went to check on a family that had been missing for days. He'd found them cowering behind the kitchen door, on which an enterprising toe-tentacled squid had stuck itself and was playing with the light switch on the other side of the room.

Another thing was haunting her, too. During the midday Bone Snatching, in which she'd nearly lost a foot, Sophie had been struck by what Ralf had said to his mother: *We're both trying to protect the same thing.* She wondered if he meant the Monster Box. Not that it mattered. She wasn't going to look for it. Not until Cartwright told her what was in it, which he wouldn't because he was a self-satisfied, irritating idiot.

Which made her wonder why she was searching the house from top to bottom, looking for a sword she could give him.

It's only fair, she told herself sternly. *You lost his in the sea.*

She entered the corridor of portraits that she saw with Scree on the first night. Almost too late she heard the stairs creak, and when she looked around she saw a shadow forming at the top of a spiral staircase. Her first thought was *ghost*, and without thinking she secreted herself behind a roll of boggy carpet leaning against the wall. Moments later the twins appeared.

"I thought you said she went this way," said Gail.

"We'll go back. Maybe she's on the beach."

Sophie pressed herself against the wall, praying to sink through the moldy plaster until they left. She watched them saunter down the corridor, until Ralf suddenly noticed the portrait of them and their father and stopped.

"So *that's* where he put it," he said. "That horrible picture. Do you remember when we had to stand there for the painter?"

"He's made that one taller," said Gail, pointing to the picture, which struck Sophie as very odd. Ralf laughed and jabbed it with his finger, leaving a small dent in his father's forehead.

"Stupid old man," he said. "He deserved everything he got. Self-obsessed, unloving . . ."

"Cold," suggested Gail.

"Yes, that's a good one," mused Ralf. "*Cold*. But never as cold as he was on the beach."

Sophie shuddered at the image of Laurel lying on the stones, an icicle on his nose.

"I sort of miss him," said Gail. "It was fun to terrorize him."

"He hated us. He called us little monsters."

"We did our best."

They stared at the portrait a little longer.

"Father's problem," Ralf said thoughtfully, "is that he had no ambition. He could make things, but he never knew what to do with them. If he'd paid attention to us we could have guided him. Turned his coffee machines into guns. We'd all be kings."

"Instead he made that stupid box."

"Cartwright should be *thankful* we're hiding it from him."

"Why don't we just throw it in the sea, Ralf?"

"You can't just destroy something like that. It's too good an invention. It could make us powerful."

"If only we had the key."

"We'll find it when we want to. Then we can use the box to make people do whatever we want. One day. When we're ready to leave the island."

"When our play's finished. But . . . maybe it won't ever be ready," Gail said hopefully.

Sophie snorted with laughter, then remembered that she was hiding and held her breath. Ralf looked around, but she was too well hidden.

"Shut up," said Ralf finally. "You're too soft, Gail."

He dug around in his pocket and came up with a pickled egg. He put the whole thing in his mouth at once, chewing while he regarded the painting.

"You're right," he said. "I *am* taller."

"Ah! Young sirs!"

Scree scuttled from the other end of the corridor. Sophie, who had almost forgotten she was hiding and had leaned out from the carpet, quickly withdrew. He ran right past, dragging a sodden mop.

"What is it?" snapped Ralf.

"I've been looking for you everywhere," said Scree. "I was mopping the ceiling, and there was an . . . incident."

"You mopped the *ceiling*?" said Gail.

"The hanging mushrooms were getting out of control," he said. "One of 'em tried to eat me."

"So what's the problem?" said Ralf.

"Some of the ceiling came down. And the plays you wrote, they've been . . ." Scree licked his lips as he searched for the right word . . . "compromised."

"Compromised?" said Ralf.

"They're wet," said Scree. "Ruined, in fact. A big inky mess mixed with plaster." If Sophie didn't know any better, she'd say he was enjoying himself.

Ralf pushed Scree against the wall with surprising strength. Scree's eyes goggled as Ralf leaned in, and Sophie fought the urge to run out and stop them.

"I thought we told you," said Ralf, "not to disturb our things."

"Her Battleshipness . . . that is, her ladyship . . . wanted me to clean everything."

"Our mother isn't in charge, General," said Ralf.

"We are," said Gail.

"Not only have you been mopping our ceiling," said

165

Ralf, tightening his grip, "you've let Silverfish out of your sight. Last night she was poking around in our secret room."

"But there's nothing secret in it, 'cause we don't have anything to hide," added Gail.

"I can't know where she is all the time," Scree croaked.

"If you let Silverfish or Cartwright poke around you're dead," said Ralf. "Do you understand? We don't want either of them finding our box."

"I don't know anything about boxes," Scree said, straining his face away from Ralf's.

"Shut up!" Ralf barked. "If you want to *keep* being a good servant to our poor dead daddy, you'll look after our best interests."

"After all, you wouldn't want us to throw you into the sea," said Gail pleasantly.

"The monsters would *love* a piece of stringy meat," said Ralf.

Ralf pushed Scree one more time, so his eggshell-smooth head hit the wall hard. Scree's face crumpled in a mixture of pain and humiliation. Sophie couldn't watch it anymore. She gritted her teeth and stepped out of the shadows, bunching her hands into fists. Scree saw her first. He shook his head.

She hesitated, her blood thick with anger, then under his gaze slid back into her hiding place.

"We'll see you later, Scree," Ralf said, and beckoned to his brother. "Let's go downstairs. She's probably in the catacombs. I've got a new game we can play with her."

"Slithery little Silverfish," Gail sang, and they danced off, clapping their hands.

Sophie ran out from her hiding place and grabbed hold of Scree, who was swaying like a man in a storm.

"You should have let me hit them!" she said as he regained his balance.

"Ha!" he barked, like she'd told a great joke. "They'd hit back harder."

"I could take them," she muttered.

"You listen to me," he said, nodding toward the portrait. "If you upset them it's both our necks on the line. They've been getting worse, and they weren't joking about throwin' me to the sea. You just let sleeping clams lie."

"Why are they so protective of this Monster Box? What's in it?"

"No idea," he said. "But it's the last thing Laurel made, Neptune rest his soul, and he was in a bad state by then. It can't be anything sane or good, that's what I reckon."

He picked up his mop and started to creak off, but then he turned back.

"The boy's waiting in the courtyard. Make sure you tell him what I just said, or we'll be nothing more than a smear on the carpet. And for the love of Neptune," he added darkly, "I don't want to be clearin' you off the walls."

"I didn't know you cared," she said, trying to hide a smile.

He scowled at her and loped away. Sophie watched until he was gone. She knew she couldn't just let the twins stamp all over Scree. Sometime soon she'd give them exactly what they deserved.

Chapter 16

Laurel's Invention

Sophie watched Master Most Violent Cartwright lounging on a deck chair in the courtyard. It was raining. Hard. Water fell from the back of the chair in a solid sheet and ran down the spine of the book in his hand. He was wearing tinted glasses, one lens cracked, which had obviously been dredged up from the sea. The blocked gutter above his head finally overflowed and dumped a load of greenish filth on him. He yawned and stretched, settled back into the chair, flipped a page over and continued to read as though he were sitting by a pool on the New Continent.

He'd been doing this for half an hour.

Fed up with waiting, Sophie flung the door open and marched toward him. The rain was so hard that within seconds it overflowed her boots.

"What's wrong with meeting inside?" she shouted through the downpour.

Cartwright held up a finger and finished his paragraph. Sophie boiled with rage.

"Can I help you?" he asked.

"You told me to meet you here!"

"Did I?"

"Yes! And just so you know," she said derisively, "those sunglasses look terrible on you."

He just smiled, like the corners of his mouth had been pinned up. Sophie looked at the book in his hands. It was upside down.

"Who's watching?" she said.

"Ralf and Gail are standing on the top floor with binoculars—don't look!" he said as her head jerked up. She saw two dim figures standing behind a pane of crusty glass. "My aunt's watching from the other side of the building. She thinks I can't see her. Just smile. And," he added, "my sunglasses look *cool*."

Sophie hadn't smiled properly in weeks, maybe months. She forced her face into a grimace. It hurt.

"They know I'm here for the Monster Box," he said. "So they're all following me around. I thought I'd make it easy for them by sitting down."

"The twins were just following *me*," she said. "They can't be in two places at once."

"Obviously you were too boring," he said, and she had to bite her tongue to stop her temper spilling out.

"Why out here?" she asked.

"It was sunny when I sat down. But they haven't moved, and I don't want to give them the satisfaction of seeing me leave first. Would you care to join me?" He gestured to a folded-up deck chair leaning against the wall.

"I'll stand." She waited for him to continue, but he just crossed his legs in that infuriatingly adult way, like he was sitting in front of his fireplace. "I'm meant to tell you to stop searching," she said. "The twins nearly bashed Scree into a thousand pieces. If you keep looking for this box he'll be in trouble, and so will I."

"The twins are going to torment you either way," he said. "You ought to make it worth your while by actually finding the Monster Box."

"I don't want anything to do with it," she said, raising her chin, but she couldn't quite squash her curiosity. "But since I'm here, you might as well have a go at persuading me."

"So you *are* interested." He sat up so quickly he nearly dropped the book. "It's quite simple. My uncle was a great inventor."

"I've seen the machines," Sophie said drily.

"In the months before he died, he became obsessed with one invention in particular: the Monster Box. He locked himself in his workshop. Before then I would spend hours every day with him, learning how to build machines and talking. He's the one who told me about the New Continent. But after he started on the Monster Box, I didn't even glimpse him."

"Right," said Sophie, refusing to appear interested.

"The evening before he died he came down to dinner— something he hadn't done in years—and made an announcement. He had finished creating something that would end the madness forever. It was the greatest, most ingenious thing he'd ever created. And he was leaving it to me."

"Ouch," said Sophie, casting another glance at the outlines of the twins.

"Yep. They already hated me, but that was the tipping point. My uncle told us that the Monster Box was locked away in his workshop, and that when he was . . . *gone*, I was to open it immediately. I think he knew he wouldn't be alive very much longer. The next day he was dead, drowned and frozen on the beach, and the box had vanished. His workroom door was splintered and hanging open, there was a square patch in the dusty floor, and there were two identical sets of footprints leading up to it. They'd taken it." His face twisted bitterly.

"And you've come to take it back," said Sophie, nodding before she could stop herself.

"But they haven't opened it," said Cartwright, "because *I* have the key. I found it under a footstool when I was searching my uncle's workshop. One of them must have accidentally kicked it when they were scrambling to get their hands on the box."

He drew something from his pocket, and it took Sophie a moment to make out what it was: a notoriously complex octopus key with eight limbs and eighty impossible-to-copy notches. He dangled it from its chain for just a second, then dropped it back into his pocket.

"The twins aren't stupid," she said. "Why haven't they stolen the key from you already?"

"They only want to keep the box away from me to drive me mad. This key is my own personal torture device."

"You're obsessed," she said. She tried to drag her eyes away from his pocket, but she wanted to see it again. "It's not healthy."

"If he left me something, it was important," Cartwright said. "He didn't do things lightly."

Sophie stepped back. She knew she was being snared by an irresistible mystery.

"I found you a new sword," she said abruptly. "It's outside your door."

"That's kind," he said. She started to walk away, and she got all the way to the door before he cleared his throat.

"It's a cure for Sea Fever," he said. "The thing in the Monster Box."

Sophie froze. Water ran off her back for a good few seconds before she turned around again. His face was utterly serious.

"How do you know that?" she asked, coming closer again. Her hands and feet felt numb.

"He said the Monster Box was *something to end the madness forever*. He'd told me once that he had a theory about Sea Fever. That the afflicted dream the memories of the sea creatures, only it's too much for humans, and it drives them mad. That's why everyone dreams of dark water and storms at sea. A disease of fear, as it were, that grabs your brain and wrings it dry of sense."

"I don't have those dreams," said Sophie.

"Neither do I. Some of us are immune. But the more I think about it, the more I believe he found a cure."

"I want evidence," she said quietly, but she knew she

174

had it already. She remembered the diagrams in the Room of Remains and suppressed a shiver.

"I found some of his notes, before the twins stole those, too," said Cartwright. "Pictures of the creatures' nervous systems, their ears, their brains. He understood them. He'd talk to them and draw pictures. I think that's what he was doing when he died."

A cure for Sea Fever. The world would be just like it was before the disease struck, before her parents really hated her. She'd be a better daughter. Tell fewer stories. She hadn't thought she'd wanted any of that, but the desire hit her so hard and so fast she felt sick.

"Think about it," said Cartwright. "We could find the box. We could leave, run to the New Continent, and cure everyone. The world would be sane again."

"Like it was," she repeated. She tried to see through the beauty of it, to find the untruth, but every part of her brain was screaming to believe him.

She forgot about how much she hated her parents. For just a minute none of it mattered. She saw the wide, seaweed-free archways of her house, the dining table laid with meals conspicuously absent of glowfish, her parents smiling when she spent a whole day being good. Maybe they missed her. And maybe—Sophie could only just admit it to herself—maybe she missed them, too. She blurted, "Fine. I'll help you find your box."

"That's the spirit," Cartwright said, grinning. "Anyway, you made your decision before you came out here. I could tell from the way you stamped out the door."

"Shut up or I won't help you at all," she said. "Tell me what to do."

"You could talk to Scree. He knows all the nooks and crannies in this place. He won't tell me anything—he hates me because I stir up the twins."

"Fine," she said. But she already had other plans. If she wanted to find the box, she had to go straight to the people who had it. She had to get her claws into the twins.

"Is my aunt still watching?"

"For Neptune's sake, you're paranoid." She looked up. "Yes, she is."

"I can't help it," said Cartwright miserably. "The other day she popped up out of nowhere like she'd fallen from the sky. And I swear Ralf was in two places at once; he was behind me then in front of me without moving."

"I think there are secret passages in the walls."

"Probably. And there's another thing. The twins went through a phase of . . . manipulating some of my uncle's machines. I think I've managed to break most of them, but if they get wind of what you're doing, they might . . ." He shuddered.

By now the rain had completely soaked her. Sophie bowed her head to stop the water getting in her eyes, and it dripped down her silvery hair and fell to the floor in sheets.

"I'll deal with it," she said. "But if we *don't* find the box within a week, I'm not hanging around. I'm taking your tickets and your horse, and if you won't help me get across, I'll force you to do it at sword point. Okay?"

"That's fair," he said.

"It is," she said, annoyed that he didn't even try to argue. He pointed at the door she just came through.

"I'm giving you directions," he said. "Nod and smile."

She nodded and smiled so hard she thought her face might crack.

"Are they still watching?" he asked.

"They haven't moved once."

"It's going to be a long day."

Sophie plowed through the rain, forced the water-swollen door open, and heaved it back with relief. She could hear the Battleship moving around on the floor above, but the twins were nowhere to be seen.

On her way back to the catacombs something struck her

as odd. She hesitated, wondering if she was being stupid. She turned and walked through the corridors that circled the courtyard, and climbed the stairs to the window where the twins were standing.

There they were, stock-still and dumb as posts, in their matching red jackets and too-short trousers. She walked up behind them and touched the shoulder of the left twin. It rocked backward and forward very gently.

Mannequins. Clever.

She peered over their shoulders at the half-drowned Cartwright. She might just leave the mannequins exactly where they were.

Chapter 17

Breaking Bones

Sophie brought the rusty ax down on a pile of scattered human bones. They cracked and shattered, yellow splinters flying past her face and hitting the wall behind her. The tunnels below were flooded, and all the bones there were floating around, impossible to reach through the murky water. It was Sophie's idea to start breaking up the bone chairs instead.

She wiped her face with the back of her hand and leaned against the ax, trying not to think about who the bones once belonged to, or whose idea it was to turn them into pieces of furniture. If she could do that, the task was almost relaxing, and it kept her mind away from the Monster Box. Whenever she thought about it she felt a bit feverish, excited and nervous at the same time. She just needed to decide where to start looking.

"Concentrate or you'll chop yer fingers off," said Scree, making her jump.

"I'm trying not to look at all these dead people."

"They're not dead people, they're chairs. It was a sort of honor, having your bones made into bits of furniture. It was so you'd be useful. Here," he added kindly. "If you stick around long enough, you can be a chair, too. I don't offer that to everyone."

Sophie shuddered. "It takes a special kind of person to think a chair made out of human bones is tasteful."

"It's not bad just 'cause you don't understand it," said Scree. "Why do you think everyone tells tales about sea draugrs? It's 'cause they don't understand the things that go bump in the night. So they turn 'em into unreal monsters instead."

"Of course sea draugrs are real!" she said, horrified.

"You ever seen one? I reckon they're big ol' fish that people see when they're drunk."

"I thought you believe in ghosts. What about the glowfish?"

"*Them's* real ghosts," he said. "Don't be stupid. Hold up, they're at it again."

There was a loud *crack* and the catacombs shook. The echo rolled through the tunnels, deep and submarine-like.

When it faded Scree began picking through the bones again, which had shivered across the floor and mixed together.

"Sounded like a big 'un," he said. "I'd go check on it, if I were you."

"Pray for me," Sophie said.

It had been pouring for hours now, all through the night and into the morning. The rain was thick and gray like a nightmare, and the sky was dumping it on the island like it was trying to wash it away. Stepping onto the oyster beach was like walking into a wall of water. Her short hair was plastered to her face, and her clothes became so heavy she could hardly walk. The sack of bones that she'd left by the catacomb entrance was gone. All that was left was a sad slip of cloth.

The culprit, a gelatinous, many-tentacled monster, flung a chunk of rock at her. It whizzed past her shoulder and smashed on the cliff face, spattering bits of black. It turned out the sea creatures didn't like the rain much. A few hours into the deluge, they had started taking chunks from the side of the island, and they hadn't stopped since.

"I know you're not really hungry," she said. "You just wanted me to come out, didn't you?"

Something fell from the sky—something small and

round and yellow-white—and hit her on the head.

She collected the missile, a mouse skull, and looked up. Something was moving on the roof. She tried to call out, but got a mouth full of water and gurgled instead.

As she got back inside, Gail slipped in behind her. He was soaking wet and looked pleased.

"Did you throw this at me?" she said, holding up the skull.

"Maybe," he said, smirking. "I'm here to give you a message. Ralf says not to go anywhere near the top of the house, because we're practicing our play and we're sick of your slimy little face."

"I wouldn't come anywhere near you if you paid me," she said as he skipped away.

Sophie went back to Scree and smashed the last of the chairs, using her scissors to hack off the lumps of yellow glue. She'd sharpened them earlier until they were as keen as razors.

The rain continued its endless drumming. One of Laurel's ceiling-dusting spiders floated out of a tunnel and washed up at Sophie's feet, upturned and wriggling its legs. She put it back on its feet and it scuttled away, brandishing a set of small wire brushes.

"Ain't seen one of those working in a while," said Scree.

"I thought they were all wound down. But who knows what's stuck in there?"

"More horrible inventions, probably. I'd love to find one that chops bones."

"That'll be why you were pokin' around the clock room, is it? Don't deny it. I heard you in there last night, moving things around."

"I didn't go anywhere last night," she said. "I don't even know what the clock room is."

"You do," he said. "Where the feeding bell is. I *saw* you. I saw you creep out of your room at midnight, all shadow-like, and I was awake so I followed, and then I lost you but I could hear you going in."

"I was asleep at midnight," she said, her mouth going dry.

"Is that so?" he said, winking conspiratorially. "Must be magic."

He nudged her in the ribs and cackled, then turned back to raking the bones into a pile. Sophie tried to keep chipping away with the scissors, but her palms were damp and they kept slipping through her fingers. One of the twins was in her room last night, making sure she wasn't up to something. It felt like her skin was trying to crawl away from the backs of her hands. The image of Ralf's or

Gail's face hovering over hers while she slept . . . *ugh!*

But then they went to the clock room. Why would they do that, unless they were checking something?

She slowly stopped scraping the bones and looked at her scissors, long-bladed and silver. She pushed them up her sleeve.

"I'll be back in a moment," Sophie said. "I need to do something."

"What's so important you have to do it right now?" Scree said. "It's coming off your tea break. Not that you get one." He cackled again, so hard he started wheezing.

Sophie hurried out of the catacombs, splashing through the stream of water that was pouring over the floor. At the top of the stairs, at the entrance to the house, someone stepped out of the shadows.

"Where do you think you're going?" Gail said, almost pleasantly.

"Upstairs," said Sophie, equally almost pleasantly. "You've obviously finished rehearsing."

She tried to walk past him, but he barred her way again.

"We told you not to go upstairs," he said. "What do you need up there?"

Sophie sighed theatrically. The cold metal of the scissors pressed against her wrist.

"There's a huge wardrobe made out of bones up there, right?" she said. "Third floor. End of the west wing. I need to smash it up, so we can feed the sea creatures and stop them from tearing your heads off."

"You don't have anything to smash it with," said Gail.

"I'm not going to drag an ax all the way up the stairs. I'll use a sword. There are hundreds of them around the house."

"Ralf would push you over and stand on your head," said Gail. "Maybe I'll do the same."

"But you won't, will you?" she said. Gail frowned, which made him look more sideways than ever. It's not that there was anything wrong with his back, Sophie realized, only that he slouched, like he was trying to make himself small. "You're not as cruel as Ralf. And you're a little bit scared of him."

"That's not true," Gail said. "Why would I be?"

"Because he's nasty," she said. "And you're not. Well, not as much."

"I'm every bit as bad as Ralf is," said Gail. "You're just too stupid to see it."

"If you say so. But right now there are creatures outside waiting to be fed, and if you don't let me get to this wardrobe they'll come through the windows and suck you and

Ralf into the sea. So do you mind?" She smiled at him.

Gail's eyes narrowed and he let her pass. Heart pounding, she climbed the stairs with the curled oyster banisters and ascended to the clock room.

After a few minutes she could hear floorboards creaking behind her, and the occasional scrape of shoes. She sped up, turning right down the corridor of portraits, and so did her pursuer, until she finally stopped and turned.

Gail pulled back into the shadows, but he was too slow, and she hauled him out by the collar.

"Why are you stalking me?"

"You're going the wrong way," he accused, jerking out of her grasp. "I was checking you didn't get lost, and you already have. It looks like you're not going to the wardrobe at all. Why would that be?"

"Get lost, you creep," she said. "I don't need you watching over me."

"Get lost," he squeaked, his face pulling itself long and frightened.

"Stop doing that!"

He blinked, then smiled horribly.

"You're still going the wrong way. Off you go, before I do something that will *really* scare you."

After a moment of hesitation she started walking back

the way she came. This time Gail didn't follow her, but she knew he'd be watching, and soon he would go to the clock room to make sure she didn't arrive a different way. She walked down the main staircase to the entrance hall, paused halfway down, and listened.

Gail hadn't come after her. She crept back up the stairs, checking at the top that Gail had moved on, and went left to Cartwright's room.

He was sitting on the bed, poring over old maps of the house. They were blurry and looked like they'd been chewed up.

"These are useless," he said as she came in. "I thought I might find a hidden room somewhere, but it's impossible to tell. I think someone drew these with their eyes closed."

"Where's Ralf?" she asked.

"Standing around the corner. He's been there for three hours. He might have the personality of a psychotic toddler, but he's certainly patient."

When she didn't reply Cartwright looked at her properly. Sophie let the scissors drop from her sleeve into her hand. Confusion spread over his face, then panic. He let go of the papers.

"Stay still, Cartwright," she said calmly.

She strode toward him. He stood so fast he knocked

his chair over, but Sophie kept going until he was backed against the wall.

"What are you doing?" he asked. "Why are you looking at me like that?"

"Run when I tell you to. Go as fast as you can, away from the clock room. Scream, that might help."

"I'm not screami—"

"Do you want me to find your box?" she said.

"Er . . . yes?"

"All right," she said, and she stabbed him in the arm with the scissors.

Cartwright screamed, long and loud.

"You're *insane*," he shrieked, clutching his arm, the scissors jutting from his jacket.

"Go!" She pushed him, and Cartwright, in a state of shock, took off, fleeing down the hallway. She hid behind the door frame just as Gail came dashing past and careered straight into Ralf. They saw Cartwright, and the blood on his jacket, and the scissors hanging from his arm, and goggled. They were frozen as he ran around the corner. They looked at each other.

"It can't be," said Gail, his fingers wriggling like he'd seen a bowl of ice cream.

"The scissor-maker's ghost!" cried Ralf.

They gave a *whoop* of delight and took off after Cartwright, their coats flapping behind them. Sophie gasped with laughter for five seconds, then raced toward the clock room before she could change her mind. She heard Cartwright and the twins running around above her, the chaos as furniture fell over.

"Here, ghosty-ghosty!" the twins called, laughing. "Give us our wishy-wishy!"

At the entrance to the clock room, Sophie rattled the door handle, looking around desperately. There was a suit of armor by the window. She wrestled its sword out of its fist and used the hilt to smash the lock on the door, once, twice, three times, and already her arms were aching. The door budged slightly, but the lock didn't give. The chase passed above her, and now it was coming down the stairs, about ten seconds away. She tried again. The door shook. She hit it one more time, feeling her shoulder crack with the effort, and then the door was open, the lock in bits on the floor.

She dodged into the cavernous, dark room and slammed the door behind her, wedging it shut with the sword. Sophie stood there, her back against the door, and breathed. She could feel things moving around her, the air thick with low trembling and ticking.

She was on a thin bridge. There was a huge void right beneath her, and catching on a thin sliver of light from the door, a sea of flashing cogs and wheels and levers. The inside of the clock room was full of sharp, brassy teeth like you'd find on a mechanical mincer.

Just as she was wondering what to do next the lights turned on, and she saw Laurel waiting for her.

Chapter 18

The Clockwork Man

Laurel was standing on the middle of the bridge, as straight as a curtain pole, watching her with his thin lips pressed together. The light above illuminated him and the grinding machinery below, but the rest of the room was swamped in darkness, making it dizzyingly huge and unknowable. Just as Sophie thought Laurel must be frozen, he blinked with a little clicking sound.

She moved forward, feeling the bridge sway beneath her, and without breaking Laurel's gaze she felt around with her hands. There were no railings on either side of the bridge, nothing to stop her from falling off the edge. She took a step forward, very slowly so as not to shake herself into the void. The bridge was about forty meters long and suspended by metallic ropes, ending on a large, junk-filled balcony on the other side of the room. Above the balcony was the greenish copper feeding bell, twice her height and as friendly looking as a beehive. Below her were the countless mechanisms of the monstrously huge clock. Cogs turned, pulleys glided up and down, and huge levers pumped and wheezed.

Laurel was holding the end of a piece of string, which disappeared through a gap in the ceiling. There was a piece of paper sticking out of his top pocket. The way he was poised, arms tensed, Sophie knew that he was there to stop people from getting across.

She edged closer, holding her arms out for balance, going farther and farther until she was right in front of him. She watched his face and searched for tics and twitches. Not one thing moved; not even his nostrils flared. His old-fashioned clothes stirred in the breeze from the clockwork, but there wasn't so much as a shudder from his raised hand. She reached out and touched his arm.

He was made of metal, a pale, cool sort that made him look alive. But his body was all wrong. It was too tall, its features too wide, its clothes cut in exaggerated flares and angles. She plucked the piece of paper from his breast pocket and opened it.

Laurel's Patent Automatic Light:
Perfect for hotel lobbies and grand houses!
Wonderful for scaring unwanted intruders!
Impress your guests with a piece of magic!
~Made to order in your own likeness~

As soon as someone opened the door, Sophie realized, it triggered the clockwork man to pull the light switch. The surprise of seeing the dead Laurel could send anyone tumbling to their death if they weren't expecting him. He—*it*—was clean and almost glowing, like it had recently been polished. Sophie had the distinct feeling that it had been placed there just for her.

She ducked under Laurel's arm, careful not to touch his uncannily cool body. His rigid arms looked tense and full of unused movement. Although his back was turned to her, she felt like Laurel was watching her with his huge, mechanical eyes. Suddenly, something swung below her with a hissing noise, and she looked down to see a pendulum the size of Manic whizzing through the void. Its passing rocked the bridge like a hammock. She took a deep breath and fixed her eyes on the distant balcony.

It was piled high with more of Laurel's contraptions, each with a small brass plate bolted to its side. Among the jumble were things that distantly looked like brass dogs, small ovens, and even a guillotine, all piled up like flotsam against the wall. Visible through a narrow passage in the junk was a door that went back into the house.

As her eyes searched the chaos her hair lifted from her neck, fluttering in the unnatural breeze. She didn't want to admit to herself that she was unnerved. She guessed she had ten minutes at most before the twins realized what she'd done and came running. She had to find the Monster Box before they followed her.

But there must have been thousands of boxes around the house in all shapes and sizes. Was the Monster Box black or blue or red? Large or small? Why hadn't she asked Cartwright what the box looked like? Come to think of it, he might not know either, which is probably why he'd completely failed to find it. He was so useless he probably hadn't even wondered.

She walked forward, knees bent awkwardly to keep her balance. Her stomach felt like it was falling out of her body with each step. Maybe she was imagining it, but the rocking seemed to be getting worse. Carefully, she looked over the side of the bridge.

The pendulum was swinging higher and higher. The last feeding was about five hours ago, which meant the next one was very soon. She could always tell when it was due, even if she'd lost track of the time, because the trembling of the house grew and grew before the bell rang.

She started forward again, knowing that when the bell struck she would be in terrible danger. Her foot immediately caught on something and she fell over. Her hands automatically reached for the sides of the bridge as her chin hit the wood.

There was a *click,* and she heard Laurel jerk his arm with a great grinding noise. The light turned off. Sophie clung to the bridge and fumbled around in the utter darkness, trying to work out what she'd tripped on, and came up against a loose plank. She hammered it down with her fist, silently praying to herself, and the light clicked back. There was a wire beneath the plank running all the way back to the clockwork man, and the decking had been loosened to make it easier to fall over. Sweeping the surface of the bridge with her eyes, she crawled toward the balcony. In front of her more planks were torn up, their edges raised to catch people, and under each one was a crudely made wire running beneath the bridge to the light switch. This must be why the twins had tampered with so many of their father's machines, to pull out all the useful bits. She thought of all the missing arms from things she saw in the Room of Remains and tried not to imagine what they could have been made into.

Whomp.

Sophie looked up to see a flat brass pendulum, bigger than the one below, cut through the air above her like a knife. She fell flat on the bridge, trying to make herself as thin as a piece of paper as it hissed toward her. The cold pendulum grazed her back, then rocketed back into darkness. She scrambled forward, clutching the bridge and sweating.

Now she couldn't pretend that she wasn't scared, because every fiber of her body was screaming at her to get out, and her chest ached with something that she realized was complete and utter terror. Box or no box, she was sitting inside a giant clock as the bell was about to strike. When it rang the vibrations would be so strong that she'd be thrown down and crushed. Scree wouldn't know what had happened to her until he found her white, splintered bones.

Whomp.

Another pendulum fell from the sky. It skimmed the surface of the bridge inches from the end of Sophie's nose, just as the first pendulum returned behind her. She was trapped between them both.

196

Whomp. Whomp.

Another swung down from the ceiling in front of her. And another. And another. Four of them in a row, released from some mechanism high above. They were swinging in time, causing the bridge to rattle like a badly tuned car. The hammer that was going to strike the bell clicked higher and higher, the sound of a roller coaster before a drop. Sophie felt the same pang of fear that she had on the tidal path, with the sea closing behind her. Her only option was to carry on.

She took a deep breath and plunged forward, throwing herself to the ground as the next pendulum flew toward her, and landed facedown on the planks.

She lay flat on the bridge as the pendulum passed over her feet and took a layer off the bottoms of her boots. She got up, legs weak as jelly, waiting for the next pendulum to disappear near the ceiling, and ran.

Things flashed past her, cogs and levers and lights and hourglasses, as the balcony loomed. Her foot caught a loose plank and she fell to the floor, cracking her chin on the wood for a second time. The lights turned out, and she could see nothing but the faint glint of machinery rotating around her. The clockwork noise was louder than ever, and the bridge was still swinging, caught between flying and stuttering.

She wanted to hurl the contents of her lunch into the heart of the clock, but she forced herself to scrabble around for the tripped wire, and when she found it she yanked it out. The light turned back on, and Sophie tossed the wire over the side.

She got back to her feet. The last pendulum came screaming toward her, and for a second she froze, her body a lump of clay. Her last reserves of logic bobbed to the surface. She threw herself backward instead of forward. The pendulum missed her head by a whisker, but the force of the movement, the air being pushed out of its way, threw her off balance. Her leg crumpled, and she slipped off the side of the bridge.

She screamed as her body slipped backward into space.

And then she was swinging by one arm over the abyss, the fingers of her right hand gripping the edge of the bridge, her hair flying around her face as a hundred bits of machinery churned around her.

She had no idea how to get back up, and it seemed that she was only putting off the act of falling. She wasn't strong enough to pull herself back onto the bridge, and her arm was screaming for her to let go.

"Help me!" she cried, her voice lost in the monstrous ticking and grinding.

On the other side of the bridge, Laurel's eyelids flicked open. As the pendulums purred around him he folded forward at the hips to form a solid right angle and rolled forth, his arms dropping with a huge *clunk* so his fingers grazed the bridge and dragged behind him.

He trundled over the bridge without pausing, squat and heavy as a tank. His timing was so precise that the pendulums didn't hit him. He didn't even wobble. Sophie tightened her grip, her shoulder burning. Through the curtain of dread, she wondered if he was going to save her.

He lifted his head and unhinged his jaw to reveal a speaker. It crackled, and there was the sound of someone clearing their throat.

"Thank you for visiting Catacomb Hill," Laurel's recorded voice said cheerily. "I hope your time here has been pleasant. Have a safe journey!"

The voice recording stopped, and the speaker spewed out tinny music, the kind you might hear on a carousel.

He pivoted to face her, so he could see her through his dark glass eyes. Sophie knew right away that he wasn't going to take her hand and pull her up; he was going to peel her from the side of a bridge like Scree would peel mussels from the rocks, then toss her to her death.

Every few seconds the swinging of the bridge made her

body jerk through the air like a rag doll, and her fingers slid a little more. The clockwork man straightened to his full height and raised a foot, his leg sliding up and into itself like a collapsible umbrella. He should have looked ridiculous, but instead he looked demonic.

He brought his foot down like a hammer, slamming it into the bridge so hard splinters flew. Satisfied, he wheeled closer to her fingers. Sophie, through a mist of panic, tried to work out how to pull herself back onto the bridge in time.

The clockwork man creaked alarmingly. Sophie swung her free arm up, her fingers just grazing the side of the bridge. She did it again, and this time she touched the leg he was standing on. His other leg folded into itself again, ready to come down on her hand, and as it prepared to stamp again she used all her strength to grab the leg he was standing on.

She let go with her other hand a split second before the metal foot smashed into the bridge, and then she grabbed that leg, too, so she was hanging with both hands from the clockwork man. He tried to fold up his legs, his machinery choking. With a sharp whine he changed tactics and wheeled away from the edge, which pulled Sophie up a few inches until she could claw her way on to the bridge.

Arms burning, chest aching, she heaved herself onto the planks. Laurel swiveled around to face her, still spewing music through his dark and empty throat.

The bridge was swaying higher and higher. She had to stay on all fours to keep her balance, but the clockwork man didn't even tilt.

Laurel's arms swung out in front of him, to push her off or choke her or whatever gruesome thing he'd been programmed to do. The hammer trembled above the bell, ready to fall with the next swing of the pendulum. With a burst of courage, she realized what she had to do.

"I hope you're watching this," Sophie shouted to the door at the other end of the room.

As the bridge swung back to the middle she ran forward and barreled into the chest of the machine. She was so light, and the machine so heavy, that it felt like she slammed into a stone wall. He jerked backward an inch. It was enough. His wheels struggled to get their grip back, and in that moment the clockwork man was hit by a pendulum and thrown off the side of the bridge.

Laurel fell down and down and down, and hit the space between two wardrobe-sized cogs. He was sucked into the middle, bits of machinery torn off and flung high into the air. The cogs sputtered and struggled. There was a large *pop* as something came loose and flew off. The whole clock ground to a resounding halt.

The bridge swung slower and slower, finally coming to rest over the jammed cogs and levers.

Sophie clung to the planks. She stayed there for several minutes, staring at the balcony. At last, legs weak and shoulders burning, deafened by the sudden and impenetrable silence, she crossed the rest of the bridge, feeling like she'd killed something.

She reached the balcony, looked up, and saw the bell hanging above her, the hammer frozen moments from striking. Still shaking, she pushed into the jumble of old inventions and junk. There were no boxes. She wriggled deeper into the stacks of machinery, but there were only piles of broken furniture. The Monster Box wasn't there. It was a theater backdrop. She had been tricked and nearly killed, and all for nothing.

Hatred rose in her throat for the twins and the house and everything in it. Sophie kicked a three-legged chair over the side of the balcony, down into the guts of the clock, watching as it smashed into pieces, splinters flying everywhere. It wasn't enough. She pushed a record player over the edge, a bunch of lightbulbs, a huge vase, a wooden mannequin, and they all shattered below. But the noise was muffled and unsatisfying. She tried to control her breathing, which was hard and painful.

As the last thing tumbled over the edge, Sophie heard it: a small *click*, like a cog or lever had shifted. A spring popped. A string was released. The balcony gently began to shake. She looked up and saw a small chain reaction travel up the side of the room, switches flicking and cords lifting on the side of the wall. And then the hammer began to fall toward the bell.

Sophie leaped toward the door and yanked the handle with both hands. It opened immediately, and she swung into the house just as the bell was struck. It felt like her head was being put through a lemon juicer. She slammed the door shut and collapsed into the cool, damp carpet of the corridor, clamping her hands over her ears until the bell stopped ringing, abruptly choked by flying debris.

Then came silence, and the house finally stopped breathing.

Chapter 19

The Bonfire

Sophie stalked the house like the Queen of Bones. Her pockets were filled with femurs; her boots sprouted ribs; her hands dripped knucklebones, which she left behind her like a bread crumb trail.

It was two days after her escape from the Clock Room, and the floodwater had finally started to drain away from the catacombs, leaving scummy tides of bones and trinkets and lost glowfish. She pushed the stranded, smashed bones against the wall ready for the next feeding, although with the house so quiet, she wasn't sure when that would be.

She'd been unable to sleep properly for the past two nights. The silence was so loud and uncomfortable that it woke her up repeatedly. She kept telling herself that it was just a house, just a clock with a big bell, and that she only felt strange because she was used to the constant, low-level ticking noise that pulsed through the walls like blood. All the same, she felt like she was balanced on a knifepoint. Unsure when their next meal was coming, the sea creatures were dangerously quiet, as though they might snap at any minute. If they got fed up and came for the house, it would be all her fault. She'd broken that clock with her stupid adventure.

She spent all morning sweeping bone fragments from the floor, then went to find Scree.

He was deep in the catacombs, hunched over a brass bowl. There was something small and squid-like inside, writhing and making little slurping noises. At first Sophie didn't think he'd noticed her.

"Sea-scrivening," he said as he stared deep into the bowl. "My old ma, Neptune rest her soul, told me anything with tentacles can tell the future. It ain't working."

"Did you get a look at the clock?" she asked quietly.

"As good as I could with a rope an' a drippy candle," he said. "Ruined. Chewed to bits." He looked at her ruefully, making her squirm with guilt. "I hope you're pleased with yourself."

"I'm sorry," she said, which she knew was a rubbish apology.

"Aye. It'll take me days to sort all the cogs out." He prodded the bowl with a long finger, then looked at her mournfully. "Maybe I won't bother. Dunno how long I'll be around."

"Don't say that!"

"Why not? I'm old. If age don't get me, something else will. I only want easy work from now on."

Sophie tried to think of something to say. Scree prodded the bowl, listening to the whistling of the squid. Then he coughed loudly. He pushed the bowl aside, pulled out his barnacle-crusted pocket watch, and held it out to her.

"Use this for the Bone Snatching," he said.

"I can't take your watch," she said, horrified.

"I don't want it anymore. The ticking annoys me."

He grabbed her hand and pushed the watch into it, his papery, calloused fingers squeezing hers tight. She wanted to thank him, but as soon as she opened her mouth he made a sound like Manic snorting.

"You're doing me a favor," he said. "I'm not long for this place. Bad things are going to happen."

"That's ridiculous," Sophie said. "You're indestructible. You're part of the house."

"Bad things," he repeated. "The twins're getting too mean even for my limits." He sucked his cheeks in disapprovingly. "I know you're looking for the box."

She thought about denying it. She couldn't.

"I don't know what's in that box, and I don't care to," Scree added. He rummaged in his pocket again and gave her the silver scissors she'd stabbed Cartwright with. "Found these on the floor. I'd hide 'em somewhere safe if I were you. Just in case of emergencies."

"What kind of emergency?" she asked, although her imagination was already running riot.

"Hop to it. It's nearly time to feed 'em." Scree pointed toward the beach, which meant she wasn't getting anything else from him.

He followed her outside and stood by the entrance to the catacombs, watching as she flung the broken bones in. As soon as they saw the food the monsters broke their silence, and they play-fought like a bunch of excitable dogs, drooling and bickering and flicking their tails at one another. Scree folded his arms and pressed his lips tightly together as Sophie threw a jawbone into the mouth of a waiting demikraken.

"Ten points," she said, looking sidelong at Scree.

"Eh?" he said. "Never heard so much youthful rubbish in my life. 'Sides," he added, "them's easy targets. You try getting a lochnessfish to catch a bone."

Minutes later they were throwing things into the sea together, aiming for the jaws of the biggest, fastest creatures, shouting at each other, getting covered in spray and foam. Scree was good; he knew each of the sea creatures inside out, what sorts of bones they liked, how they moved, how high to throw; but the creatures vied for Sophie's attention, crowding around her feet to get the next mouthful and, she swore, doing watery acrobatics in front of her.

"There it is," said Scree, wiping the sea from his eyes. "You've got something about you. Me, I think they're a slobberin' bunch of children, but they know you're soft for 'em deep down."

"I'm not soft for them," Sophie said, scowling. "I'm not soft for *anyone*."

"'Course you are. I should be a bit proud of that, if I were you. Mind you," he added, "it won't stop 'em from eating you. They like something, they want to chew it up all the more."

Secretly she did feel proud, in an odd way. She felt like the sea creatures were hers now. As she walked back to the catacombs she almost thought that everything was going to be all right, and that the island wasn't such a bad place after all.

And then she saw what had been left for her.

There were two scraps of gold placed casually, almost as if by accident, on the slab of rock she called her bed. Her fingers went cold as she walked toward them. They looked like small coins—as if someone had given her a present. But then she was close enough to pick them up, to press the gilded paper between her fingers, and she knew that it was no gift.

They fluttered down, the bits of paper with spidery black writing, and she was gone before they reached the ground. On her way through the tunnels she almost knocked Scree over, but before he could complain she was racing into the house with a scream of fury building in her throat.

"Ralf! GAIL!"

She was answered by a silence so deep it must have been deliberate. But there was something else: a smell, and it wasn't damp, mold, or seawater. She could smell smoke. It curled through one of the windows, creeping in tongues past a crack in the frame.

She pressed her face against the dirty glass and squinted. The twins were in the garden, their red heads bobbing up and down as they dragged bits of dead tree around, building a den or something.

A bonfire.

She ran to a rotting door, fury surging through her whole body. She rammed it open with her shoulder and went through headfirst, landing in a knot of brambles, her foot still caught on the threshold. She turned over like a fish on dry land and tried to free herself, then rolled sideways into a patch of stinging nettles, and cursing, spitting leaves, stumbled off into the garden. She sprinted toward the plume of smoke, which was coming from the pointed end of the island.

Twenty yards into the garden, which was more like a forest, she could hear distantly triumphant crowing. The twins were singing now. She could hear them perfectly. And then she burst into the clearing where the bonfire was. The twins were each holding a ticket to the New Continent, waving them close to the flames like they were toasting marshmallows.

She went straight for Ralf, who sidestepped her so neatly she plunged into the ashes and the bottom of her trousers caught fire.

"You must have been running fast," said Ralf.

"Where did you get those?" she gasped, trying to beat

the flame out. She swiped for Ralf's ticket, but he grace-fully lifted it out of her reach.

"These?" said Ralf. "We just found them. Funny, the things Cartwright keeps in his sock drawer."

"Do you even know what they are?" she said. "You wouldn't be waving them around like that if you had any sense in your thick heads!"

"No idea," said Ralf. "But they're obviously valuable to you. To Cartwright, too, seeing as he'd installed a booby trap."

"A loaded crossbow behind the door," said Gail. "How very unoriginal."

She lunged for the ticket in Ralf's hand. He *tsk*ed and raised it again. He was taller than her, very tall indeed, she realized, like he'd grown overnight. The ticket gleamed above his head.

"Jump for it," he said. "Go on."

"All right," she said, and stamped on his foot. She grabbed his elbow as his face creased up and tried to snatch it from him. Gail coughed politely, then started to shred his ticket.

The sound of ripping went on forever, as painful as if Sophie were having her nails pulled out. Gail put the torn corner in his palm and blew it into the bonfire. The paper crackled and sparked.

"Here's the thing, Silverfish," said Ralf as he raised the ticket above his head again. "All this sneaking around is amateur. Playing tricks, creating decoys, follow-me, follow-you, et cetera. That was Act One. We should move on now."

"You're going to rot under the sea," she hissed. Her fury was so strong she felt like she should be able to lift the island from its foundations, to strike both the twins to the ground with one blow. She snarled and swung her bunched fists, but Ralf caught her arm and twisted it behind her so she was trapped. When she was fighting someone she normally won by ignoring the rules and kicking right where it hurt. But the twins knew how she fought, and they were just as good at it. She couldn't hurt them by playing dirty.

"Tut," said Ralf. "We expected more of you. Isn't that right, Gail?"

Sophie twisted her arm out of Ralf's grip, but he caught it again. She saw Gail wince. It only took a second, but his face told her everything she needed to know. She realized Ralf had done exactly the same thing to Gail, time and time again since they were little.

Ralf pushed her closer to the fire, so close that she couldn't see anything but impossibly bright light. It scorched the side of her face, her lips drying like bits of paper, her eyelashes singeing. She'd never imagined being burned to death before, but now the possibility was so frighteningly close that she saw in a flash how it would happen: She would go blind, and her skin would burn, and her bones would crack in the heat. She wanted to believe that Ralf wouldn't kill her, that he didn't have the guts, that she was just being frightened by a stupid game; but the flames were hot, and she couldn't reason her way out of it.

"Take a good look at what you're doing, Gail," she croaked. "Standing there, watching Ralf hold someone over a fire. Don't you think you'll get what you deserve one day? Do you think it'll be nice?"

Gail looked miserable. "Ralf, I don't like this game. You said she'd be easy."

"Stop being such a soggy mattress," snapped Ralf.

"It's 'wet blanket,' you idiot," Sophie snarled at Ralf, and regretted it immediately.

Ralf twisted her arm and she screamed, then she bit him on the hand and he let go. She rushed to Gail, about to grab the ticket from his limp hand, but he caught her with the same surprising strength as his brother.

"As I was saying," Ralf continued as though nothing

had happened, "I think it's time we moved to the next act. You want something that we have, and we don't want you to have it. But the odds, dear Silverfish, are heavily stacked in our favor. We're clever, and strong, and cunning and . . . clever. You're not going to win. Sooner or later, we'll end up having to get rid of you. But first, we're going to play a game."

"I'm sick of your games," she said. "Your father would be turning in his grave."

"He doesn't have one," said Gail. "Silverfish, you broke our toys. And the robot man. We spent ages on the clock-work room."

"Gail did all the tricky wiring," said Ralf. "He's very upset. What are you going to do about it?"

Sophie was struck by the same weird feeling she'd had when she was hiding behind the roll of carpet, the twins looking at their portrait. It was like they'd let their masks slip.

"I'm going to break everything that you send after me," she said. "Machines, knives, fire, whatever. And now I know exactly how you work. The whole thing was a decoy, wasn't it? You knew I was going to break into the clock room, so you set it up especially. But why go to all that effort?"

"Fun," said Ralf, flashing his nails so she could see how sharp they were. "What else are we meant to do around here? You've been entertaining. You even tricked Gail to get into the clockwork room, and he's usually a wonderfully loyal guard dog."

"What, I wasn't really guarding anything?" said Gail, looking briefly poisonous.

"Of course you weren't. You're *useless*."

"You're sick," Sophie growled.

"*You're sick*," mimicked Ralf, twisting his face so for a moment she was looking into the eyes of her own doppelgänger. For someone who was bad at acting, he was sometimes shockingly very *good*.

Sophie stepped forward, and Gail, muttering angrily about Ralf under his breath, let her go.

"I'd like to know," said Sophie quietly, leaning in close to Ralf. His eyelids flickered, and she knew he was just a tiny bit perturbed. "There must be a reason you put so much effort into tormenting me. Why are you so scared of me? Is it because I'm cleverer than you, or is it because you know I'm going to beat you?"

From the corner of her eye she saw Gail's face change. He was terrified of what was going to happen. He looked at his brother as though Ralf was going to eat a puppy.

"Scared," repeated Ralf. He rolled the word around his mouth as though tasting it for the first time. So close, his breath smelled disconcertingly like peppermint. "Scared . . . no, I don't believe I am. This island is our world, and we pull all the strings. It's our universe you're stepping in." He leaned in as well, so his nose was grazing Sophie's. She felt a wave of nausea, but forced herself not to withdraw. "You've opened the floodgates now, Silverfish."

She looked right into his sharp blue eyes, forcing herself not to blink.

"Game on," she said.

Ralf gestured to Gail and he snatched both of her wrists up, holding them in a tight, twisted grip. The moment shattered, and Ralf looked pleased again.

"As I was saying," he continued, "we're going to play another game with you. Scree managed to ruin our script, so we need a little help reconstructing it. You're going to be Ophelia, Silverfish. Say your lines."

"I don't know any lines."

Ralf raised the ticket to his mouth, tore a lump off, and chewed slowly.

"I don't know any lines!" she screamed.

"Get them right or I'll swallow all of it."

As her fury spilled over Sophie realized she'd had a plan all along. Without thinking she drove her elbow into Gail's stomach, and he made a soft noise that sounded like *oomph*. With her other arm she reached behind her and snatched the torn ticket from his clammy palm. Gail dropped to his knees, wailing. Ralf ran at her, but in the two steps it took him to reach Sophie she'd ducked under his outstretched arm and risen behind him. He stopped for just a moment, and his hesitation was long enough for her to throw her weight into the center of his back. He made a noise like his brother and also dropped to his knees.

"You little ball of slime!" he shrieked. Sophie grabbed the ticket from his hand. Both the twins were back on their feet now, and they moved so that Sophie was sandwiched between them and the fire. The smile on Ralf's face grew bigger as the flames scorched Sophie's back.

"You've got gall, I have to admit that," he said. "If you weren't a girl, I'd almost want to be your friend."

"You wouldn't," she said. "Trust me." And then she jumped into the fire.

Gail let out a strangled scream, but the sound passed her by as almost incidental, something outside of her world. There was a searing flash of heat, a wall of hot air. The sound of flames breaking and cracking the broken furniture under her feet. For one moment she thought she'd made her final move. But then she was out of the fire, and running, trailing sparks and charcoal behind her.

She used to play with candles when she was little. She'd swipe her fingers through the flame, thinking how like a magic trick it was that she wasn't burned. It didn't scale up so well. She could smell her own burnt hair and the bottoms of her trousers were on fire again. Her feet felt like they'd had knives stuck through them. But the bonfire wasn't as big as it was in her imagination, and if she had anything it was speed. She'd outsmarted the twins again.

Then she remembered the tickets between her fingers, and looked down at her hand, which was empty. She opened her fingers. They were stained gold. A thin strand of paper withered and curled in on itself, turning to ash. The rest of the ticket, black and burned beyond recognition, fluttered out behind her like moths.

It was very quick, the total destruction of hope.

She staggered to a halt and reached out for support. She hung on to a thick, black branch, half-wreathed in smoke. Behind her, the twins cackled.

"Silverfish loses this one," said Ralf, his voice twisting through the gloom. "But there's a bonus round: Silverfish now realizes she's been a pawn all along."

The forest grew bigger and darker. A spider dropped onto her forehead, and she let it slide down her nose. Her skin was numb.

"The bonus round ends," continued Ralf as his brother giggled beside him, "when Silverfish asks Cartwright what happened to all the other servants. I suspect she's been avoiding the question, dear audience. She knows that there have been many boys and girls on the island before her, but does she know that they've all helped Cartwright look for his box? *Everybody* loves Cartwright."

Gail clapped his hands delightedly.

"You've done well, Silverfish," continued Ralf. "You've done *much* better than any of the others. But your end will be just as sticky as theirs."

"They ran away," Sophie managed to say, through teeth that seemed to be cemented together. She couldn't feel or hear or see. "They went home."

"They definitely tried to," said Ralf. "But did they make it? How hungry do those monsters look to you, Silverfish? Did those other servants actually get across the water? Do you think we would let them get away that easily?"

"Poor Silverfish," said Gail, not without some sadness. "Look at her. I think she's crying."

"Let's leave her be, then. All alone, out on the island where nobody loves her."

"How sad."

"How sweet."

"Maybe she really *will* go mad and drown herself."

"We can only hope," said Ralf, "that we'll be there to watch."

Chapter 20

All of Them Eaten

Cartwright was picking his nails with a piece of glass. He was in his bedroom, one long leg draped over the other, perched on a velvety chair in front of a dusty mirror. Sophie opened the door so hard it bounced off the wall, and although Cartwright didn't jump, she saw that his fingers had slipped and there was a small drop of blood hanging from the end of his thumb.

When he realized who it was he grabbed the first thing that came to hand, a silver hairbrush, and held it up like a weapon.

"Put it down," Sophie commanded. "Drop it!"

"Drop it? You psychotic, stabbing, scissor-wielding—"

"Shut up," she said, and much to her surprise he did. She snatched the hairbrush from him and flung it across the room. Something smashed.

"I think you owe me an apology," he said, folding his arms.

"You're a liar, Cartwright. Everyone told me you were trouble, and I ignored them. But it was true all along. You're a dirty, cheating, scummy *liar*."

"What have I done?"

"The deal's off. I'm not helping you find the box anymore. I wouldn't help you if you paid me."

"I have no idea," he repeated, leaning away from her, infuriatingly calm, "what you're talking about. Have the twins done something to you? Whatever they've said, they've done it to make you angry. Besides," he added, "we have a deal. You need a ticket."

"There are no tickets," she said. "Happy? They were burned."

"The twins burned them?"

"They *got* burned."

Cartwright smirked.

"So *you* destroyed them. How did you manage to do that?"

"It's not funny," she hissed, and Cartwright scrambled up and backed against the wall as she marched right up to him. "I don't know why you're sniggering, because it means you can't go to the New Continent either."

"I'm not laughing," he said, holding up his hands. "In fact—"

"Don't change the subject!" The anger rose again, hot as a spill of lava. "The twins did say something to me, actually. And I know they were telling the truth, because suddenly it all makes sense."

"Maybe you should sit down," suggested Cartwright.

"Maybe you should be quiet and listen," she said.

"Will you stab me if I don't?"

"I swear to Neptune—"

Cartwright dodged her fists, which were raised to hit him. "Fine! I'll listen."

She glared at him and sat on the bed, right next to the sword he kept hidden under the duvet. The sword *she* found for him. Cartwright, eyeing her like she was a wild animal, removed himself from the wall.

"People have been working here as Bone Snatchers ever since your uncle died," she said. "They get sent over, Scree trains them, and then one day they disappear, leaving behind little notes telling your aunt that they've run away. It makes sense, because who would want to be here unless they had no choice?"

She glared at Cartwright until he nodded again.

"But something you forgot to mention," she said, "is that

every Bone Snatcher has been doing the same thing as me, looking for this Monster Box. Every time a new one comes to the island *you* conveniently appear and offer the same deal. A box for a ticket. And when they disappear without finding the box, you wait for another one to turn up."

"All right," said Cartwright. "You're not the first. Maybe I should have mentioned that. It was a bit unfair of me, but—"

"There's more," she said, tightening her hands on the bedcovers. "I saw their running-away notes the day I came here. I knew there was something weird about them, but I was too naive or stupid to see the truth. They didn't run away, Cartwright."

"Of course they did," said Cartwright. "They disappeared in the middle of the night, as soon as the tide was low."

"The tide's only low twice a year! I know you can storm over it on your mad horse, but what chance does anyone else have? There's no boat and there's a pack of monsters baying for blood. There's no way dozens of people decided to casually stride across."

"What are you trying to tell me?" said Cartwright. He had his arms folded, but there was a hint of panic that he couldn't quite hide.

"The notes are fake!" she said, her voice rising uncontrollably. "The twins were pushing them into the sea! All those people are *dead* because of you, and you're too stupid or immoral to stop it happening again!"

"I'm not immoral!"

"Did you ever read the notes?"

"My aunt had them all."

"How convenient!"

"I would *know*," he said, standing up. He took the piece of glass from the dresser and fiddled with it nervously. "Ralf and Gail are little monsters, but they're not capable of killing anyone. Can you actually see them doing it? They play with their food, for crying out loud."

"I think they're worse than that," she said. "I think they're only pretending."

"Pretending what?"

"To be idiots."

She could see the color draining from his face.

"You've got to believe me," he said. "I thought they went back to their homes. I *still* think that."

"You're not thinking hard enough."

"I wouldn't have asked for help if I thought anyone was going to get killed, Sophie."

"Don't try to be *nice*."

"Just listen! Have I ever suggested you do something dangerous? You're the one who went poking around the clock room. You're the one who antagonizes the twins, and it's you who stabbed me with a pair of scissors! You want to have an adventure, because it's more of a life than sitting around and taking your pet poodle for walks or whatever you did at home. Admit it. You *enjoy* all the near-death experiences."

"I didn't have a pet poodle," she snapped. "And stop trying to twist your way out of this."

"If I didn't care at all," he plowed on, "would I have come after you in the night when you stole Manic? He came back to shore by himself. I could have left you there in the sea, and as you so eloquently put it, waited for another one to 'turn up.'"

Sophie slowly released her grip on the bed. She wanted to believe him. He was as wriggly as a ferret, but for some reason she wanted to think he was a good person.

"Are you going to ask about the tickets?" she said.

"Do I want to know?"

"Ralf and Gail stole them. I managed to grab them and escape through a fire—yes, you heard that right—but they were completely destroyed. There's no New Continent for either of us, just the same old world we're used to, box or no box. I mean, really. Your *sock drawer*?"

"They've never done that before," he said quietly.

"Once is enough," she said. Scree's pocket watch began to play a jolly tune, an old ditty about a drunken sailor, vibrating and clicking against her heart. She'd have to feed the monsters in fifteen minutes.

She bared her teeth at him, channeling her inner sea creature, and left.

The catacombs were bare, all the bones sucked to the bottom like they'd gone down a drain. The bits of smashed-up bone chair had disappeared. The creatures had already eaten them, boldly creeping into the caves and drawing them into the sea.

As the watch played its tune Sophie ran onto the beach and started shoveling stones into the water, but the monsters didn't want stones today. They converged on the oyster racks, pulling the last spindly legs into the water and crunching the barnacle-crusted wood noisily. The tide was a long way out, like the sea was taking a huge breath. Another storm was on the way.

Sophie paced the shore. She didn't know what to do. She couldn't get to the New Continent because the tickets were gone. The monsters were getting hungry, and she was running out of bones. And she felt stupid, really stupid, for not wondering what had happened to all the Bone Snatchers before.

Even Scree hadn't said anything about it. That hurt most of all. He must have known all those people were disappearing under weird circumstances, but all he said was to *be careful*. She'd started to think of him as a friend, but she felt bitterly hurt, no matter how hard she tried not to think about it.

For the first time in a long while she felt tears pricking her eyes. She wiped her face with the back of her hand and swallowed. Crying was stupid and it didn't achieve anything. But all the same, her eyes kept leaking.

She shoved her hands in her pockets and walked along the beach to distract herself, looking for scraps that she could toss to the monsters. She noticed a row of pearls by the shore. Curious, she edged closer. The monsters were too busy with their feast to bother with her. She picked the shining object up and dropped it with a yelp. Sitting by her feet was a row of false teeth, large and polished, a shining half grin. She would know those teeth anywhere.

There was a low gurgling from the sea, and an accusatory, pointing tentacle lashed out fast as a whip, grabbed the teeth, and dragged them under.

"Oh, Neptune," she whispered to herself. But surely the sea monsters would never catch Scree—he was fast and wily, despite his aching bones. And he knew the monsters inside out. Maybe he'd dropped his teeth. She'd probably see him wandering around later, poking the shore with his grab-claw contraption.

She heard a low crunching behind her and spun around, expecting to see a crab chewing stones. Instead she came face-to-face with Cartwright. Gone was the tall stance and cocky smile. He looked . . . sorry.

"What?" she said rudely, trying to cover up the fact that she was disturbed.

"That's a rubbish way to say 'hello' to someone," he said. "If you weren't so intent on being aggressive you'd have heard what I was trying to say earlier. About the tickets."

"I don't want to hear it," she said. "I just want to be alone."

"Have you been crying?"

"Do you want a broken foot?"

"You should try being nice sometime."

"So I've been told," she snapped. "Why are you out here?"

"To explain myself," he said. "You owe it to me to listen, if only because you stuck those scissors in my arm. When they were chasing the ghost Ralf leaped on me from a chandelier and almost broke my back. Gail tried to chew my ear off! I'm serious."

"What do you want to tell me?"

"A story."

"Is it a true story?"

"As true as the rocks we're standing on, but told with style and vim."

"What's the point?"

"To elicit your sympathy."

"I don't have any."

"What if I told it anyway?"

"I don't promise to listen."

"I knew you'd say that," he said, and sitting on a rock he began.

Chapter 21

Another Sad Story About an Orphan
In Which the Dazzling Cartwright Strikes the World

Ladies and gentlemen, humans and creatures, monsters and men: what follows is another sad story about an orphan, one of the many left behind in the wake of Sea Fever. The unfortunate boy's name was Master Most Violent Cartwright.

Young Cartwright, eight years old, was shipped off to his uncle's oyster farm with a suitcase containing a change of clothes, a toothbrush, and a packet of biscuits. He was bedraggled, upset, and pitiful, but really quite handsome. Now that I think about it, it's a shame he wasted his childhood on that dismal island when the world could have known his uniquely dazzling personality. Are you laughing? Don't laugh. Now, where was I?

His new home was haunted by his vicious cousins, Ralf and Gail, who spent their time playing cruel but uninventive tricks on him—flushing his head down the toilet, stealing his books, hiding fish under his pillow, and so on. Cartwright would have thought of more original pranks himself, but he was better than that, obviously. And he wasn't the only one subjected to this terror. His uncle, Laurel, an inventor of the highest order, was also tormented by his sons. Laurel's wife, Agatha, directed the twins toward him like a hunter with a pack of dogs, furious that her husband wasn't, in fact, interested in her.

Here our story intersects with another; let us go sideways, like a boat slipping gently into a current, to the story of Agatha Fischer, a woman who married Laurel for his oysters. Having brought up twin sons with a penchant for making others miserable, she was more than slightly regretful when her husband was driven to an early grave and the torturers turned their attention on her. Her three emotions are consequently guilt, loneliness, and stone-shattering fury. But Agatha would do anything to protect Catacomb Hill, as it's the only thing she has left, though secretly she hates it so much she wants to see it destroyed.

But let us veer back to the dazzling Cartwright and his similarly tortured uncle as they bond over their shared passion for hiding from the twins. Laurel told Cartwright stories about the stars and planets, about all the different countries, about the sea and the things that lived in it. That's how Cartwright heard about the New Continent. The boy was hooked on the posters and maps Laurel brought back from the mainland. He'd never seen anything so full of promise. When his uncle, who was already pretty old, started going a bit—How should I put it? Crackers?—it seemed like the stories of the New Continent kept him going.

But let's not forget about the twin monsters living in the house. They hunted Cartwright with a passion, and they started to sabotage Laurel's inventions in the middle of the night. They put a hole in the boat and pushed it out to sea. Laurel started to go madder than before, and Cartwright suspected that he had finally succumbed to Sea Fever. One day, Laurel locked himself in his study and didn't emerge for two months. All he told Cartwright was that he had found the cure, and it was his duty to see it made reality.

Laurel created the Monster Box and left it to Cartwright. It was obviously Cartwright's destiny: he would travel to the New Continent and give his uncle's legacy—most certainly a cure for Sea Fever—to the world. Everything would be all right again, and our dazzling orphan Cartwright would be a hero.

The rest, dear audience, you know. The twins became jealous. They stole the box, and Cartwright, in the throes of grief, took the key and fled the island.

Cartwright knew he needed to get himself on a boat and to the New Continent, but despite his most admirable talents, he had no way to buy passage across the sea.

Now twelve years old, he joined the army. They were only too glad to recruit him on account of his obvious talent and maturity, although many have said that they were also desperate for men. Because he was quick and clever, and because the others had either gone mad or fled, he was soon promoted to captain. He rescued a manic horse from a burning tar pit, and became known as the most unpredictable, intimidating man in the force. Soon he had enough money to get tickets—two of them, in fact—one for himself, and another in case he ever needed a bribe.

But he couldn't stop thinking about the Monster Box. He got angrier and angrier at the twins. They had cheated the world out of a cure for its malady, and they had taken something that was rightfully his. He wanted that box.

He took off in the middle of the night. Tickets in hand, he reached the coast and rode across to the derelict oyster farm.

The only thing that had changed in the house was the ad-

x

234

dition of a servant who helped Scree with the Bone Snatching. He asked for the girl's help, and in return promised her passage to the New Continent with him. She accepted, but just a week later she disappeared, leaving a note to say that she had run away for London. Cartwright, feeling claustrophobic, left the island again. He traveled up and down the country, doing circus tricks for peanuts. The tickets were always in his pocket, but every time he determined to board a ship and leave the country, the itch to take back what was rightfully his made him step back.

So he returned to the house. There was a new servant by now, who also agreed to the deal, but the same thing happened again. He left, and a few weeks later he was back, and there was another Bone Snatcher.

He was exhausted and obsessed. He tried to grow a fashionable beard several times. And he was beginning to really worry about the twins. He wondered what they had to do with his uncle's death. He wondered what they had to do with the disappearing Bone Snatchers. He wondered if he was lying to himself. He vowed to go back one last time, to confront the twins and his aunt himself, if not to find the box then to say good-bye to the island and his uncle's memory. This time he meant it.

There was a new servant, a girl with white hair and a pointy face. She looked about as abandoned and hateful as he felt. At dinner, he turned to the girl. Old habits die hard, and the great pretender Master Most Violent Cartwright struck again.

Chapter 22

Feeding Every Kind of Creature

"One small secret," said Cartwright.

He reached for his inside pocket and pulled out a brown envelope, which he handed to Sophie. She tore the end off. Two gold-colored tickets slipped out. She held them up to the light as though they might disappear, but there they were, solid as the stones that were digging into her legs.

"The twins didn't burn the tickets," Cartwright said. "They burned the decoys. I made them as soon as I got here. There was gold paper in the library, and I only had to write on them in black ink. I put them in my sock drawer. I thought the twins might go looking for them, and I was right. Obviously they fell for it. So did you. They think they've broken you now, so they'll leave us both alone for a while."

"You had the real ones all along?"

"I keep them on me all the time. And now one of them is yours. I don't want you to think I'm a total horror. I'm trying to do better. Keep the ticket, and if you want to leave, I'll put you on Manic tomorrow, and you'll never see this place again."

She studied them closely. She wanted them to look fake, but they didn't. These were thick and heavy, perfectly printed. More like tickets than the things the twins had.

"When I ran away the first time," she said slowly, "and you dragged me back, I'd stolen a ticket from your sock drawer. Would it have gotten me anywhere?"

"You had a bad fake," he said. "They would have laughed and turned you away."

"You made me feel so guilty about it!"

"Your intention was still rotten."

Something was occurring to Sophie for the first time. Her fingers loosened on the tickets.

"I don't know if I really wanted to leave anyway," she admitted.

"What does that mean?" asked Cartwright.

"I kind of like the sea, and even the creatures. I'd rather be on Catacomb Hill than trying to get on a boat. This doesn't mean I've forgiven you," she added. "I will still despise you forever, eternally, until the stars burn out and Neptune comes down and freezes everything into a block of ice."

"You're so angry all the time. All you do is stomp around and threaten people. Doesn't it get tiring?"

"You'd feel like this too if your parents shipped you off to an island of death while they went on an extended holiday."

"I rather think mine did," he replied.

"But did they hate you?"

"I don't think so. They just didn't *like* me that much. There's a huge difference. I doubt your parents actually hated you either. Maybe they were scared of you, or they didn't understand you."

"How wise of you," said Sophie. She sighed. "It was my toes that scared them. I think they suspected I was a changeling."

"What do your toes have to do with it?"

Sophie pushed her boots off and wriggled her twelve toes in the gravelly beach, grinning. Cartwright stared.

"Maybe it's why the sea creatures like you," he said. "You're a defective human being."

"It's also where I get my superior, cat-like balance from,"

she said, then remembered that Cartwright was a lying coward. "I'm going. I need to get more bones for tomorrow."

"But what now?" said Cartwright. "Are you leaving? Aren't you going to demand I take you across to the mainland?"

"Not yet," she said, looking out to the flat, black sea. "I'm going to stay for a couple more days. Not because I owe you anything. But I feel like there's unfinished business. Like something's going to happen, and if I don't stay to watch it, I'll regret it for the rest of my life. I'm doing this for myself."

"And you want a cure for Sea Fever."

"Yes. No. *Yes.* If we could undo it, the world would be . . . better. And my parents . . ." she trailed off. She didn't know what she was going to say. That they'd be proud of her? Want her back? Did she even want *them* back?

"It's contagious," said Cartwright. "The feeling that we're on the edge of something. It's this island. It gives me the creeps."

"It is creepy," said Sophie. "But it's more than that. It's like I know something important, but I can't quite worm it out. I'm missing something. Something *huge.* And I can't leave until I know what it is."

"You're the weirdest girl I've ever met, Sophie Seacove."

"And you're the most blatant flatterer. You don't have to be nice to me."

Cartwright looked at her with an expression so unfathomable the only thing she could do was stare. She saw that there were tiny freckles on the side of his face like new constellations. Then she wondered why she was noticing them.

"Got to go," she blurted. She got up and hurried toward the catacombs. Cartwright shouted something at her. But soon he was far behind her, and his voice was lost in the roar of the sea.

It was night again, and Sophie's breath rose in white plumes above her. Funny how she couldn't sleep now unless she was on a slab of rock. She'd tried settling on one of the damp, marshmallow-like mattresses upstairs, but it felt like she was being engulfed, and she had nightmares that she was back at home in her old bed. Down in the catacombs the eerie singing of the wind felt like a lullaby. As she drifted off she thought of the New Continent. There was something about the idea of the pristine isle that had begun to disturb her. Maybe she was just used to Catacomb Hill, with its strange moods and unpredictable personality. She tried to fix the watercolor of trees in her mind, the one that was on all the posters, but it swam away as soon as she got near.

Morning broke slowly. Sophie got dressed and washed her face in a snail-filled pool of water. She listened carefully for Scree, who at this time of morning was usually pottering around with his fishing contraption, telling her to hurry up. The tunnels gaped at her like empty mouths. She didn't know where Scree slept, or ate, or spent his time when he wasn't polishing the rocks or fishing. She wondered if he was in the clock room, tinkering with the mashed-up cogs and levers, but she was sure he would have told her.

Scree's pocket watch made a sound like it was clearing its throat and started playing. As the song wound down, and she overcame the urge to smash the thing to pieces, four round eyes appeared in the entrance to her hovel with two sets of white, shiny teeth.

She tried to slip into a gap in the wall, but the twins had already spotted her.

"Get out!" she shouted.

"We want to," said Gail sulkily. "But everything's gone wrong."

"Oh, has it?" she hissed, picking up what she thought was a rock but turned out to be a clump of socks. "How terrible for you."

She expected a comeback, or a small act of violence, but the twins didn't come any closer.

"We're hungry, Silverfish," Ralf said instead. "We want breakfast."

"Scree didn't make dinner last night," said Gail. "We can't find him. We haven't eaten in over a day."

"We get annoyed when we're hungry," said Ralf, stepping closer. "I went *mad* the last time Scree was late with breakfast, didn't I, Gail?"

Sophie tried to push past them, but they held their arms out and herded her back into her cave. A spasm of fear went through her. She was alone with the twins, where it was dark and nobody could hear them. She imagined the other Bone Snatchers going through the same thing, person after person being cornered in the catacombs, the twins reaching out with their sharp nails and frozen smiles. She picked up the only thing she could find, a broken fishing rod, and advanced.

"She looks angry," said Gail. "She must've fallen out with Cartwright."

"Must have found out what a sneak he is."

"Why is she grinding her teeth like that?"

"She's a girl. They're all irrational."

She dodged under their arms, and they followed as she

ran all the way out of the catacombs and into the house. Their images flashed past in the tilted, broken mirrors of the grand entrance hall. They ran lightly and silently in a way that reminded her of daddy longlegs, their limbs stretched and lanky, their feet barely brushing the carpet.

"Mummy!" Ralf bellowed, and as Sophie leaped over a broken vase she came face-to-face with the Battleship, four heads taller than her, voluminous skirts extending on either side of her like wings. The twins overtook her and hid behind their mother, peering out from their barricade.

The Battleship stared at her, small black eyes sunk deep into her pale face.

Then she sucked her cheeks in and raised her hands, which held a knife and fork in each.

"Kippers and mash," she said. "You're the cook until the General decides to do his job properly." She took a deep breath. "YOU'RE ALREADY FIVE MINUTES LATE!"

Sophie tried to formulate a response, gave up, and ducked past the Battleship's skirts toward the kitchen. The twins cackled behind her, and she could hear the dining room doors opening, the Battleship settling into her creaking throne.

It was clear that the stove had been cold for a long time. Sophie searched through the cupboards and shelves, which were jammed with bits of rusting metal but very little food. She pulled a huge stockpot from underneath the sink, got a flame after five broken matches, and dumped in a dried fish, some grayish soup from a tin, and one of the sprouting potatoes by the sink. As soon as it started to bubble she stuck a ladle in it, heaved the pot onto the floor, and dragged it behind her, leaving a groove through the small passageway to the dining room.

The twins hurled themselves upon it like they'd never eaten before, digging out lumps of potato with their fingers and smearing gray soup over their faces. The Battleship picked the pot up like a cup and poured half of it into her mouth to which the twins, now in a good mood, clapped and yelled "Bravo!"

"Disgusting," muttered Sophie, edging out of the room. Ralf leaned back in his chair and burped.

"Sleep well, Mother?" said Gail sweetly.

"My mattress is lumpy, as you well know," she said, casting him a stormy look. "I haven't slept well in years."

"The princess and the pea," said Ralf, and smirked. "I wouldn't complain about it. Bad things happen to those who complain."

The Battleship picked a fish bone from her teeth and closed her eyes.

"It's like there's a ghost watching me every step of the way," she said. "I try to crush it under my weight each night, but it doesn't work. And I dream that if I pry it open and look it in the eye, everything will be blown apart, and this terrible place will be smashed into the sea."

As she finished speaking she opened one eye and stared directly at Sophie. Sophie froze, halfway out the door. She was sure that the Battleship was trying to tell her something. The Battleship, irritated by her slowness, picked up her fork and slowly bent it in half, grinding her teeth like she was trying to work something out.

"Oh, do shut up, Mother," said Ralf.

The monsters were in for a treat today. Sophie took the pot to the oyster beach, spilling the remains of the gray gunk over her foot as she went. She set the pot sailing into the sea, but before it had traveled three feet it was pulled under, and a dull ringing noise came from under the waves as it was crushed.

"You like it?" she said to her unlistening audience. "Well, we're running out of bones, so this is what you're getting from now on. Slops. You'll be more thankful than them anyway."

Now that the pot was gone, tentacles rose from the

water and began waving at her, accompanied by a long, angry trumpeting.

"There's nothing left," she shouted through the din. "Maybe some bones deeper in the catacombs, but I can't do everything at once, and you've got to be *patient.*"

One by one the creatures withdrew their tentacles, except for the scaly demikraken, which was slithering toward her. She stepped back too late, and it reached out with its barbed claws.

"Don't you dare!" she spluttered. As she tried scrambling away she willed the creature to recognize her, but it seemed to have no idea who she was—as though she hadn't fed the monsters three times a day and played games with them.

"It's me!" she shouted, but her voice was lost in the seething water.

Its teeth were wide and shining, and it kept getting closer. Sophie swept her arms over the stones and grasped the handle of the crushed stockpot, which was as flat as a tennis racket. Without thinking, she twisted her body to avoid its grasp and smacked it over the head.

Its eyes wobbled. She heaved the stockpot over her shoulder, prepared to fight it off, ready for truly earthshattering rage, but nothing happened. The monster folded up with a whine and withdrew into the sea.

The rest of the creatures slinked back and collected in the shallows again. Sophie quickly got up and backed away from the water. They all stayed there and watched her, almost like they were waiting for her to do something. Like they were *nervous*.

She knew she should be annoyed with them. But with the purple tentacle marks that still blazed across her back, the welts on her arm, and her weird hair and extra toes, she thought she was a bit of a monster herself.

"Don't try to eat me again," Sophie said. She took a deep breath and tried to make her voice stronger. "If you do, I'll knock your teeth out. Do you understand?"

There was a small commotion in the middle of the crowd, and one of the creatures brought her a dented tin of oysters with the label sucked off. It spat it out at her feet. She picked it up and held it uselessly as creature-slobber dripped down her arm. She got the weird feeling that they were waiting for her approval.

"Thank you," she said. She put the tin in her pocket. "It's . . . great."

There was a joyful hooting sound, and with a great roar one of the creatures flung something at her. Sophie picked it up, her stomach plummeting. It was Scree's fishing contraption, splintered and covered in tooth marks. Dread washed over her.

They waited for her to do something else, but she turned her head so they couldn't see her expression, which she could no longer control. She slowly crunched back to the catacombs, the fishing contraption clutched in her shaking hand. At the entrance of the cave she looked back but the creatures had gone.

Everything looked flat and calm, like she had just woken from a dream. Her heart gripped against itself in a way that made her feel weirdly sick.

The monsters had eaten Scree. It felt like the world was falling away from her, and tears pushed against her eyelids again, so heavy that she had to hold them in with her fingers. It was even worse knowing that the monsters likely didn't know what they had done.

There was nothing she could do to help him. Finally, for the first time since she had arrived on the island, she sat down and sobbed.

Chapter 23

Dead Girls Mess Up the Carpet

The evening descended quickly, gobbling up the sun long before dinner. Sophie didn't really notice. She'd spent the day raking the catacombs for Mister Scree, feverishly hoping that she had been wrong and he was alive. It wasn't until the moon was fully visible that she found his room in the tunnels.

It was tucked around bends and corners, half camouflaged behind an old net, lit by a natural chimney that twisted up and into the garden. A grandfather clock with a mechanical bird inside trilled as she entered, the bird swiveling as though to watch her. Scree had very little else: just a neatly made camp bed and, on a small table, a cold mug of tea and a half-eaten bowl of porridge.

Seeing a grubby piece of paper on the table, she picked it up and held it to the light. It was some sort of diary.

09/18: Creatures ate my gloves and spat out a load of gobbins. Shouted at them but got a stone lobbed at me.

09/19: Calm sea today. Looks like the demikraken has toothache. Ralf pretended to be Laurel, scared me from my old bones.

09/20: Monsters tried dragging me under again. Found a demikraken tooth. Boot stolen by flatfish.

09/21: Choppy waters. Losing favor with them. V. tired.

09/22: Fought with the giant squid. Nearly had my teeth. Twins tried to push me into the water. Creatures chomping their jaws at me.

09/23: Girl turning up today. Neptune help us.

He'd written in it every day without fail. She flipped the paper over and read his increasing fights with the sea creatures until the end, where it cut off two days before now.

"They ate him," she whispered, feeling hollow. "They ate Mister Scree."

That evening they held a funeral for him, just her and Cartwright standing on the beach with a sputtering lantern. She didn't ask him to come, but he turned up anyway, like he knew what had happened. Maybe he'd been watching from his window. The creatures had taken a huge chunk of rock from the outside wall of the catacombs and flung it across the stones, so Sophie and Cartwright stood on it with Scree's chewed-up fishing pole as Sophie tried to say a few words.

"Well," she said, voice wobbling a little, "our good friend Mister Scree's gone. He'll be missed terribly." She stopped. It sounded too stiff. If Scree were there he'd snort and tell her to get on with it, and anyway, it was weird to be talking about him in the third person. "Look," she said, raising her voice. She waved the fishing contraption. "Scree, I don't know if you had any friends or family outside of the island—I guess they'd all be dead by now anyway—but I'm sure you were thought very highly of."

"You made interesting food," said Cartwright solemnly. "And you were always on time."

"Right. And you were very good at fishing and polishing your stones. I'll try and keep them sharp, but I can't make any promises. And I'm still sorry about the bell. I suppose I'm trying to say—"

"*Bon voyage*, Mister Scree," said Cartwright. Sophie threw the fishing contraption into the water, where it was snapped up by the jaws of a large fish.

For the rest of that evening Cartwright helped Sophie

dredge up bones from the deeper parts of the catacombs, and she showed him the glowfish scales plastered on the walls. They hid the bones in sacks out of sight of the beach, as she suspected the creatures would snatch them otherwise. When they dumped the last sack on the floor, hands red and blistered, there was an uncomfortable silence. Cartwright looked at her like he was waiting for her to say something. She stared at him awkwardly, trying to work out what he wanted, until it felt like she was drowning.

"I'm sorry I stabbed you with a pair of scissors," she exploded.

"What?" he said.

"And I'm sorry I stole your horse and lost your sword. And took your tickets. And broke into your room. Lots of things, really."

"Oh." He looked surprised, then quickly wiped it away. "It's what makes you so delightful," he said graciously.

"I mean it. I'm trying to be a Good Person."

"That was a very convoluted way of saying you're glad you met me."

"Will you let go of your ego for one second?"

A groan echoed toward them as though a large faucet had been turned on. They stared into the mouths of the tunnels, and just as it seemed that they imagined it the noise happened again. It sounded like someone was dragging things around.

"Is someone down there?" Cartwright called, drawing his sword.

"Scree said there were sometimes squid in the pipes. Or maybe it's his ghost."

"There's no such thing as ghosts," he said, but he sounded rattled. "The twins?"

"They've never been down that far. There's nothing but glowfish. What about the Battleship?"

"She never leaves the main house. She'd only come down here if Ralf and Gail made her."

There was a pause as they listened, but the tunnels were silent again.

"What do you mean?" she said finally.

"She's scared of them. She'll do whatever they say. You know, I actually feel sorry for her." He squinted at her through the gloom. Sophie was shaken by the feeling that the answer was very close, the location of the Monster Box just out of her reach. If only she could *think*. "What's wrong?" Cartwright asked.

"I need to work something out."

"You're as pale as an eggfish."

"I've got to go. I've got to get up early, to feed the monsters and make breakfast and . . ." She backed away. Her head was crowded with thoughts, and she had to make sense of them before they slipped away. "I'll see you tomorrow."

"What have I done now?"

"It's nothing!" she yelled. "Nothing at all!"

She ran back to her room, trying to untangle the puzzle before all the pieces flew away.

That night Sophie dreamed of storms and shipwrecks, monsters and men, and the dark, turbulent breathing of the catacombs in the howling wind. The Battleship's doughy white face kept rearing up in front of her, those raisin-black eyes squinting into her own and her small, red mouth opening in a howl of frustration. And then it sank, again and again, into the dark ocean of Sophie's dream.

In the early hours of the morning the wailing sea creatures woke her, and when her eyelids opened at last, she knew the answer was on the tip of her tongue.

She stared into the shapeless gloom. A thought was clamoring to get out, but she struggled to collect it until an imaginary phantom seized her by the collar.

"I sleep on fear every night," the Battleship said, holding her aloft. *"My mattress is lumpy. I haven't slept well in years. It's like there's a ghost watching me every step of the way,*

and I try to crush it under my peculiar weight at night, but it doesn't work."

The phantom disappeared. The wailing had stopped, and Sophie was flat on her back on the bed of rock, sickly light filtering in from the house upstairs.

"It's under her bed," she said. She heard herself and sat upright so fast the room began to turn. "She's sleeping on it!"

She fell off the bed and shot straight toward her shoes, an unfamiliar grin spreading across her face. It was so obvious. If you had something really precious, where did you put it? Under the bed, with your favorite toy that you were too old for. The twins, no matter how clever they were, were still children with childish ideas. And the Battleship, scared of her sons and of Cartwright finding the box, let them keep it there. No wonder she was so angry when Sophie went in her room.

If she wasn't so happy she'd kick herself for being so slow. The Battleship had been trying to tell her. She wanted Sophie and Cartwright to find the box. If Sophie found and stole the Monster Box, it wasn't the Battleship's fault. She wouldn't have to look after it anymore.

Sophie struggled into her clothes and rushed, boots unlaced, to Cartwright's room. Fleets of tiny ghost-fish skidded from under her feet, dodging between the suits of armor, as she splashed across the hallway. She half expected the twins to step out and grab her, but it was too early for them to be awake and she was, at least for now, safe. She raised her fist to hammer on Cartwright's door, but it swung open at the first touch.

Cautiously, she poked her head into the room and saw Cartwright sprawled facedown across the bed, arms hanging off the side and fingers touching the floor. His skin was white and he wasn't moving. Stifling a scream, Sophie went to the bed and tried to see if he was breathing, but he was still as a corpse and she thought there was a bluish tinge to his fingers. Had he been poisoned? Stabbed? Were the twins waiting behind the door for her now, holding darts in their fingers?

Then Cartwright, still pale as whitewash, emitted a huge snore and rolled over. Sophie swiped a glass of water from his bedside table and emptied it over his head.

"Back away!" he screamed, in one swift movement both sitting bolt upright and drawing his sword. "I'm armed!"

"It's me, you idiot," she snapped, and he dropped it.

"What is it with you creeping around my room when I'm asleep?"

"You need to get up," she said. "Grab anything you

need and get ready to leave. I'm getting the Monster Box for you."

"You're—what?"

"No time to explain," she said. "Get Manic and wait by the entrance."

"Where is it? Let me get it!"

"You're like a bull in a china shop," she said as Cartwright fumbled for his octopus key and dropped it. "I need to sneak in and out of a room. Trust me, you won't get anywhere near it."

It looked like Cartwright was about to argue with her, but he knew she was going to win. Sophie touched the ticket to the New Continent that she kept in her inside pocket, next to Scree's pocket watch. She was so close. Once the box was found, she'd be able to start living a real life on the New Continent. The Sea Fever would be cured. And they'd both be free of this terrible place forever.

"Give me ten minutes," she said. "And for Neptune's sake, put some clothes on!"

Leaving Cartwright riffling through his drawers, Sophie slipped back into the hallway and started the ascent to the Battleship's room. She'd been in the house long enough to know her way, and she made sure to avoid the twins' rooms and any creaking floorboards that might wake them. The Battleship only left her room at very specific points in the day: thrice for meals, and very early in the morning, long before breakfast, to stand at the front of the house and regard the sea with her tiny, staring eyes.

On the top floor of the house a new gray morning was filtering through the broken ceiling. Just as Sophie neared the room the Battleship's door creaked open. Sophie wrenched open a large wardrobe that smelled of mothballs and shut herself inside, breath caught in her throat. Through the crack in the doors she watched as the Battleship emerged, silent as a ghost ship, her tiny slippered feet making the faintest marks in the carpet. The woman came toward her, paused outside her hiding place, and sniffed the air. Then she carried on, only the faint groaning of the stairs marking her passage.

Sophie closed her eyes and forced herself to count to ten. When she could breathe normally again she slipped from the wardrobe and into the Battleship's room, closing the door behind her.

She'd imagined that it would be easy to find something as dramatically named as the Monster Box, but there were so many drapes and scarves and furs, so many stuffed animals, jewels, candles, stacks of paper, mirrors, clothes, shoes, and dead flowers that she had to look hard for the bed, the outline of which was blurred by the piles of rugs on top of it. Sophie picked her way over the crowded floor and kneeled down. She could hear something scuffling around under there, and when she tentatively lifted the edge of the duvet a mouse shot out and disappeared into a mound of junk.

It was hard to see anything. Sophie lowered her head, choking a bit on the dust, then crawled entirely beneath the bed. The hard wooden floor scraped her knees. She came up against a pile of shredded bedding, presumably left there by the rodent, and a dozen or so damp books that served to prop the bed up—but there was no box, nothing even vaguely box shaped.

She knew she must have missed something. She tried to loosen some of the floorboards, but they'd clearly been nailed down for years. She raised one by a few inches but it snapped back with a noise like a gunshot. She clapped a hand over the vibrating board, going cold at the thought of the twins hearing.

But nobody came. She felt stupid about her idea. Who actually hid things under the bed, anyway?

"Is there a magpie in my room?" the Battleship boomed

from the hallway, barely five feet away. "Is there a little birdie flapping around the windowpanes?"

Terror seized her. Sophie tried to get out from under the bed, then realized that the Battleship was about to come in and she would be trapped. She fumbled her way back under, cracking her head on the bed frame. Just as she pulled her feet under, the door opened and the Battleship oozed in. From the shadow on the floor Sophie could see her head swivel like an owl's, surveying the land. She sniffed again like a hunting dog.

"My sight and hearing are bad, but I can smell a thief from a mile away. Where are you hiding? What are you looking for?"

Sophie could smell it herself, the scent of fear and unwashed feet, the mustiness of the catacombs that now seemed to be a part of her bones, the fish she'd been eating at mealtimes. But maybe it was a trick—something to frighten her and flush her out. *Let it be a trick*, she begged to herself.

"Found you," said the Battleship, and as Sophie tried to squirm farther away a hand grabbed her ankle. She scrabbled at the floor, catching splinters of wood under her fingernails as she was dragged out. "Slithery little fish. I warned you once."

Sophie was hoisted a few feet above the floor, upside

down, her silvery hair falling over her face like a curtain.

"I came to get the Monster Box!" she gasped as the room swung around her.

"What makes you think I'll give it to you?" the Battleship said incredulously, shaking her like a bag of coins. "Who are you to take it?"

"I know you want me to find it."

"UNTRUE!" the Battleship screamed, and threw her down. Sophie hit the floor with a *crack* and scrambled into the corner, head ringing.

"It's driving you crazy," she said. "I can get rid of it."

"You won't take my house away from me!" the Battleship yelled. "I married Laurel! I put up with him even when the oysters disappeared, and then I put up with his boys! I deserve to keep the house! I've worked for it!"

"I don't want the house!"

The Battleship lunged toward Sophie, but Sophie was quicker, and she threw herself toward the bed as her attacker plunged headfirst into the wall. The Battleship got up and swiped her huge paw at Sophie, who dodged the blow, wriggling off the bed with her teeth bared. She ducked again and again as the Battleship tried to snatch her, until they were almost at the door. But just as she was about to grab the handle a blow caught the side of her head, and she was knocked across the room into the half-open window. The room swayed and her legs turned to jelly as the Battleship advanced, blocking Sophie's escape route. She could feel the air at her back and the empty drop beneath her, a hundred feet or more, right into the sea and the crooked rocks and the salivating creatures below. Her stomach plunged, but she looked the Battleship straight in the eye.

The Battleship shook her by the shoulders.

"Any last words?" she said. "Anything you want to say?"

"Yeah," said Sophie as the windowsill hit the small of her back again and again. "I'm sorry for you. You should have left this place years ago, but you were too scared. Now you're stuck, and it doesn't matter who you throw out of your window because you'll never leave!"

"Too late for words," said the Battleship. "Gobble gobble! The monsters are having girl for breakfast."

Sophie was snatched up by the neck and suspended over the windowsill. Her heart was bursting out of her chest, and she could no longer pretend that she wasn't scared, because this was it. She was going to die.

And then she saw it. A corner sticking out of the pile of rugs at the top of the bed. Enameled blue, with a twisted, many-mouthed lock peeking out. And even as she started

263

to black out from the pressure of the grip around her neck, Sophie felt a wave of sadness for the woman who used the Monster Box as her pillow every night.

"So close," she mumbled. After all this, Cartwright would never know where the box was, and the world would never be rid of Sea Fever. It was so horrible it was almost funny.

"What?" the Battleship asked, lowering her slightly. Sophie's feet found the windowsill, and she managed a strangled breath. Her sense began to return. She dimly remembered that she always had one weapon on her, but she couldn't remember what it was.

"What?" the woman barked again, shaking her so hard she bit her tongue.

Ow, she thought. And then: *Ah.*

"I win," Sophie said, and sank her pearly teeth into the Battleship's wrist.

The woman yelped and dropped her, and Sophie only just had the presence of mind to grab her huge pearl necklace to keep herself from falling. The Battleship shrieked and stumbled back, shocked by the thing hanging off her, and Sophie dropped to the floor and grabbed the box.

"GET BACK HERE!" the Battleship shrieked as Sophie raced through the door with her prize.

She plunged down the corridor, sending up spray as her

feet hit the floor. The Battleship was close behind, blocking the light and coming at her like a landslide. Sophie leaped down the stairs to the entrance hall three at a time, falling over at the next landing, and scrambling away just as the Battleship's hand grazed her ankle. Every inch of her was focused on reaching Manic, and as she neared the entrance hall a ferocious triumph overwhelmed her. She was almost there.

She swung round the corner at the bottom of the next set of stairs, just missing a suit of armor that she hadn't known was there. She stumbled, just for a second, then instead of passing the door she raced into an unfamiliar corridor crammed with junk.

Sophie almost dropped the Monster Box when she realized what she'd done. She'd never seen this hallway before, and the carpet looked like it hadn't been walked on in years. There was no room to turn back with the Battleship on her tail, so she kept going. She skidded into a dead end, and stopped, furious at her own stupidity. She bent over to catch her breath, aching with despair. The Battleship slowed to a walk.

"I am sorry, little magpie," the Battleship said. "When you catch a fish, you ought to bash its head against the floor to stop it from suffering, but dead girls mess up the carpet.

I'll have to decide what to do with you later. Don't make any noise or I'll do something nasty. I don't want the boys to know you got your hands on their box."

Sophie, with a burst of anger, leaped up and tried to push past her, but the Battleship jerked her foot and sent Sophie sprawling. With her foot planted firmly on Sophie's back, she threw a painting off the wall, revealing a huge door with a handle in the shape of a gargoyle. Sophie tried to squirm away, but it was no use. From inside her dress the Battleship drew a bunch of keys, selected one, and twisted it inside the lock.

The room inside was completely dark, and as unknown and terrifying as the inside of a sea creature's stomach. Sophie felt her mouth turn dry.

"I'll take that," the Battleship said, removing her foot. She stooped to wrestle the Monster Box from Sophie's arms, lifting her up as she clung on.

"Give it back," Sophie spat. But the Battleship shook her off, then gave her a small nudge that sent her sprawling into the dark room.

"You won't have to wait long," the Battleship said. "Careful of the sharp things."

The Battleship wedged the Monster Box under her arm and locked the door, leaving Sophie in darkness.

Chapter 24

The Obvious Untruth

In Which the Power of a Story Is Revealed

From the way her breathing filled the space Sophie knew that she was in a cramped, junk-filled room. After the Battleship had trundled off down the corridor, everything was silent. Every time Sophie moved there was a stirring along the wall, a fluttering motion like it was covered with sleeping bats. Was there someone there with her? She held her breath and the feeling ebbed away.

Cartwright would be wondering what had happened to her. Maybe he'd come and find her, and she'd tell him where the box was, and they could grab it before anyone knew she'd escaped. Unless the twins had already found him waiting by the door with Manic, in which case he was done for. And even if he did come looking for her, why would he come to the end of the lonely corridor, and pull this painting off the wall, and even then how would he open the locked door?

Sophie held her hands out in front of her and stepped forward, trying to find a lantern or candle. She walked straight into a metal contraption with levers and rollers that felt like a giant typewriter, and got her hand stuck in it. There was a brief struggle with the machine before she pulled herself free. As she stumbled her hand brushed over a brass plaque, which she pressed under her fingers to read.

Laurel's Patent Printing Press
Where the Stuff of Dreams Is Made!

She pulled her fingers back like they'd been burned. Nothing good had ever happened after finding one of Laurel's inventions. She moved away, meeting the wall, which was dry and flaking, with bits of wallpaper peeling off like scales. She cautiously ran her fingers over the paper, and found a small metal switch.

She had no idea what to expect, but her curiosity won and she flicked it anyway. She covered her eyes as a dim glow filled the room, coming from a glass bulb in the ceiling. When she was able to see she wished she hadn't flicked the switch at all.

The whole room was gold, its walls and ceiling plastered with individual pieces of paper that gleamed under the lightbulb, each one pinned in place with a thumbtack. There must have been thousands of them, each with the same spidery handwriting which made it look like there were immense black cobwebs stretched over everything.

She squeezed her eyes tight shut, and the part of her brain that saved her in the clock room, the part that made her bite down on the Battleship's wrist, said insistently, *Look again!*

She did. The walls were plastered in precious, priceless tickets to the New Continent. Sophie reached out, blinded by a mix of horror and disbelief, and tore one down. She tried to look at it properly, but there was something wrong with her brain again, and the words were wriggling under her eyes like bits of rope.

She put her head in her hands, trying to think.

These tickets looked just as real as the one Cartwright had given her; identical, in fact. She stared at them both side by side, then got confused as to which was which and stuffed them both in her pocket. She turned, and walked right back into the mangled typewriter which seemed to have crept up on her.

It had a sheet of gold leaf hanging out of it, abandoned

midway through printing, and next to it was a guillo-tine for slicing the paper into rectangles. But there was more stuff still. There were maps and pictures and adver-tisements that had drifted across the floor, and a huge, squashed chair. She grabbed a piece of paper and read an advertisement for the New Continent, but half its type had been crossed out and corrected. Why was Laurel copying posters as well?

She let go of them. They skidded across the floor. She knew that something was terribly wrong, and the truth was bearing down on her like a steamship.

Under Laurel's squashed armchair was a book. Sophie picked it up and found herself looking at Laurel's diary. She sank into the armchair and opened it to the first page. At first it was filled only with diagrams and comments about his machines, and some references to Cartwright and the activities of the twins. Then there were some longer passages, which Sophie skimmed through, until the words the *New Continent* caught her eye. She flicked back with shaking fingers and began to read.

I got carried away. I thought it might give the boy something nice to think about, and indeed, after telling him about the New Continent there was a vim in his step that I hadn't seen before. It made me feel a lot better about his being trapped here with me. Even the twins, who are growing more malicious every day, can't make me feel downhearted now that Cartwright is happy. And now—on with my inventions!

There were a few more pages with writing and diagrams of the many-limbed coffee machine, which in the pictures was smiling, then:

We talked about the New Continent again, and I got rather excited. Later, I had a bright idea—why not make everyone else smile, too? I looked at the wind-blasted town on the shore, and thought about the eyesore I had built in their sight line and the monsters I have drawn here with my oysters, and thought I could make up for it. Neptune knows they could do with a smile.

In other news, the twins tried to make me watch a play. When I finally sat down they spent ten minutes shouting at each other. I'm finding it difficult to hide my distaste for them.

She skipped the next few paragraphs, which detailed the twins' movements, and came back to:

. . . I distributed a pile of posters for the New
Continent around the town. As soon as I got back I
regretted it, because they will know who did it and think
me at best mad, at worst a fraudster. On the other hand,
it should make the townspeople very happy. And there's
nothing I can do about it now. Onward!

Sophie's mouth was dry. She had the feeling that her mind
was skimming over something obvious. She prodded it like
a rotten tooth, but she couldn't pin it down.

I had to go to shore to see to some financial business,
and I was cornered almost immediately by a gang of bad-
smelling bandits.
They asked if I had left the posters for the New
Continent, and proceeded to demand that I tell them
how to get there. I was going to explain everything,
but they hit me in the face before I could finish, and
threatened to come for my family.
I am not worried about Agatha or the twins, who
would tear the heads off of anyone who came close, but
young Cartwright, who I think takes after me in my
brilliance and intellect, must not be harmed. Next week

I will come back with a "map" to the New Continent,
which in reality will lead to nowhere. Luck willing they
drown in the ocean, the scoundrels.

I finished my coffee machine the other day, but for
some reason I can't get its face right.

There were some more diagrams and a picture of a
squid. Sophie didn't want to keep reading, but her hand
had a mind of its own, and she turned the page.

Blast! The scoundrels who cornered me started selling
copies of my "map," and now half the town has gone.
There has even been a spate of boat thefts! I went to find
the mayor to warn him that his citizens were taking part
in a scam, but he was apparently one of the first to leave,
citing the need to take charge of the New Continent
before a less scrupulous mayor could seize power. Now
the office is being held by a twelve-year-old boy. I asked
him if anyone had come back from the New Continent,
and he said, "No, sir, but I suppose that's because they're
having such a good time."(!!!)

One of the maps has got into the national newspapers,
and now shipping companies are selling tickets to get
people there. People are feverishly fighting for them in the

streets, and there had been more than one murder. But
I have an idea—I can produce my own tickets, flood the
market with them, and stop everyone fighting. Problem
solved!

    I have decided that Sea Fever must have played a part
in all this, and that, as a side effect, it turns its victims into
half-wits.

Sophie dropped the book onto her knees. Her hands were cold. She riffled through the pages, past more diagrams.

    It's this place. It makes me do things. Catacomb Hill
is my prison, and my terrible family are the jailers.

    The shame I feel at my fib is growing. My ticket plan
isn't working, even though my press is churning them out
day and night.

    To distract myself I am working on my latest
invention with renewed vigor, before I am totally lost to
insanity, or the monsters, or, Neptune forbid, the twins.

The next few entries had huge smears across the page, as though water had dripped onto them. The next legible entry:

My new invention is almost complete. A machine of immense power but brilliant simplicity. It's the only thing that can bring an end to the madness. It will doubtlessly fix the mess I've made.

The last entry was a scrawl.

It is late. The twins are lurking outside the door. I have the dreadful sense that something terrible is about to happen.

I may not have time to confess to Cartwright that the New Continent is not real. It was a story just for him, one spread by my posters in a moment of madness.

This is my full confession, and may it damn me forever: I have sent thousands of people on a one-way trip to the middle of the ocean, and Neptune himself couldn't bring them back.

There is no New Continent.

Everyone who has made the journey is dead.

Chapter 25

A Ghost in the Catacombs

Sophie threw the book down, trying to block everything out by stuffing her fingers in her ears. It fell open on a diagram of a huge, mechanical eye. It stared at her as the revelation oozed through her mind; she tried to keep it out, but the horror seeped over like a sea creature forcing its way into an oyster.

"They're dead!" she cried, throwing herself against the wall. She tore into the tickets hanging there, then grabbed whole fistfuls of them and ripped them down, losing herself in a papery snowstorm. "My parents are dead. They're floating under the sea like eggfish. Oh God oh God, they're all dead, my neighbors and everyone are dead, and *I* wanted to go there, *idiot.*"

She spun around and toppled the printing machine, ripping levers and cogs out with her bare hands, her voice rising to a scream. She didn't care who heard her now. Everything—all of this—all for *nothing*! Laurel had sent thousands of people to their deaths, and she'd been living on the dream of a sham paradise. It all seemed so obvious now, the stupid pictures of pink clouds and green fields, the promise of fresh fish and somehow, no rain—*how could she have been fooled like everyone else?* Laurel was mad, and the Sea Fever epidemic had helped his ridiculous stories spread. And it all started here, in this room, with this terrible, insane old man trying to convince his nephew that the world was a good place, when all he'd done was make it worse. Sophie kicked a last frame into the corner, where it broke in two. She wondered if Cartwright might have known all along about the New Continent and the fake tickets. He wasn't stupid. He knew his uncle was loopy. Maybe he'd been stringing her along on false hope to get what he wanted. The Monster Box. The cure.

As Sophie fell silent, exhausted and choked-up, she heard the Battleship stomping down the corridor.

She shoved some of the tickets into her pocket, in case she needed them later, and cast around for a weapon. The bits of machinery were too heavy to lift, so she settled on a piece of broken picture frame and stood by the door, the light turned off again, the piece of wood raised above her head.

In the dark, behind her eyes, her parents stepped onto a boat with their suitcases and hat boxes, and the gangplank drew up, and the ship pulled out of the harbor, and Laurel laughed.

The floor creaked. The vision cleared. Outside a key turned in the lock, and the door swung open.

"I'll dash you against the floor for making such a racket," the Battleship said, framed against the light.

Without pausing to think Sophie swung around and whacked the Battleship in the chest with her weapon. The huge woman groped in the air for her invisible assailant, and Sophie shoved past her, throwing the wood aside and sprinting into the hallway. She'd been running so much that every piece of her ached like a broken instrument, un-tuned and ready to snap. But still she carried on, making no mistakes this time, trailing golden tickets like messages until she reached the main staircase and hurled herself down.

The main doors in the entrance hall were ajar, and Cart-wright sprung through when he heard her coming. She could hear Manic huffing behind him, kicking the ground and complaining.

"Where were you?" he said. "You've been gone almost an hour! I thought there was something wrong!"

In a split second she had to make a decision: trust that Cartwright was another victim, or throw him into the sea for lying about the New Continent. Her mouth opened and words got stuck in her throat. She just didn't *know*. But she couldn't steal the Monster Box back by herself.

"Your aunt's chasing me," she said, clinging to the doorknob. "The box is in her room. She's using it as her pillow. When she's gone past, run up and get it—"

An infuriated roar echoed through the house, shaking drops of water from the ceiling.

"—while I keep her distracted. I'll meet you out front. Be quick!"

She pushed him out the door so he wouldn't be seen, just as the Battleship started thundering down the stairs. Sophie took off again. There was no time to consider whether Cartwright would actually stop for her when he had the box; she just had to trust him. She pounded across the carpet and plunged into the black catacomb tunnels.

The Battleship stopped at the throat of the caves and opened her mouth.

"RALF! GAIL!" she screamed. "THE RAT IS ESCAP-ING! GET HER!"

Sophie threw herself around the corner and pressed herself against the wall, trying to make room to think.

"Don't worry, Mother," said Ralf, stepping out like he'd been waiting around the corner. "We'll take it from here."

"Yes," agreed Gail, sounding peculiarly unlike himself. "I think it's time to end it all."

Sophie ran her hands over the rock beside her. Her scissors were hidden deep in a crevice, where she'd put them after Scree's warning. It was like he knew that one day Sophie would be waiting in the tunnels, needing something sharp and dangerous. Her fingers touched a piece of cold metal, and she drew out the same silver blades she'd stabbed Cartwright with.

Strange how she felt so calm now, like she was only heading, slowly and inevitably, toward whatever destiny Neptune had mapped out for her.

She put the scissors up her sleeve. It was time for the final act.

The twins tapped past her, their footsteps echoing into the caves. Sophie was pressed into the rock, and the cata-combs embraced her. She was a piece of stone, and she felt as cold as the heart of the Glowfish Pits. When the twins had gone past she removed herself, pulling her damp skin away from the sticky rocks, and followed.

"Silverfish," Ralf cooed in front of her. "Where are you, pretty Silverfish?"

They padded deep into the throat of the largest tunnel. Ralf gestured to Gail to strike a match, and a sudden flare of light illuminated the catacombs. Gail swept the match around so the shadows of stalactites swung across the floor, then Ralf saw what he wanted. It wasn't Sophie.

Gail blew out the match and dropped it.

"This way," said Ralf, and they walked off.

When they were a few yards ahead of her Sophie followed. The whisper of her boots was like a shout, the *snick, snick* of her heels as loud as a series of gunshots. Together with the twins their feet made a kind of hideous song. But they were focused only on what was in front of them. She fell into their pace, touched the cold blade under her sleeve, and waited for the right moment.

"Again," said Ralf. She drew back as Gail struck another match. "This way," he said, and the match was dropped. Their heels ground as they turned ninety degrees, pivoting neatly on the spot, and continued down another tunnel. They were following something on the floor, but she couldn't see what it was without a light.

"Again," said Ralf, and this time Sophie was caught by surprise and she was nearly too late. She pulled herself into a shallow nook just as the match flared. She was closer to them than she thought, and their shadows touched her feet. The smell of sulphur reached her nostrils. As the light dipped out she saw what the twins were following: a set of fresh, wet footprints.

Something was wrong. Down here footprints stayed for two, maybe three minutes before they shrank and disappeared, and she knew she'd been the last one down here, over an hour ago. They didn't look like any prints she'd seen before; she could only imagine that someone had dragged their feet, slowly and heavily, over the rock. They looked like draugr prints, the footsteps of the cannibalistic undead.

The twins set off again, this time a little quicker. They worked silently, making no noise but for that of their footsteps. Down here they weren't even arguing with each other. This, Sophie realized, is how they acted when they thought they were alone.

"I heard something," said Gail, and they stopped dead. This time they were too quick for her, and as Sophie's feet scuffed the floor the twins took a sharp breath.

"Silverfish," Ralf cooed. "Come into our net, pretty little Silverfish."

There was nowhere to hide. Gail struck a match, and in the flash of light she saw them facing her with their larger-than-life smiles. They were now three feet away from her, watching her like a moth trapped against a pane of glass.

"Gotcha," said Ralf. Gail held the match between his thumb and forefinger, shrieking with laughter like a hyena.

"When this match goes out," said Ralf, "so do you. Won't that be fun?"

Sophie tried to slide away, but they started walking toward her, perfectly in time and smiling. She braced herself for a fight, letting the scissors slide down her sleeve and into her hand. Then she saw what was behind them, and a sickening chill ran down her spine.

Something dark grew out of the rocks behind the twins. At first it looked like another shifting shadow, but it loomed up until it towered over the twins. Sophie managed another strangled sound, and Ralf laughed. A greenish hand reached from the darkness and closed on his shoulder.

She had just enough time to see his eyes widen with fear, and then he was pulled back from the light. Sophie turned and ran. Ralf screamed, and so did Gail, but then he started running, too, leaving his brother howling, dropping the match which extinguished with a hiss.

Blind again, Sophie stumbled toward where the house should be, but in the dark it was impossible to tell what she faced or was running into. There were gaping pits in the floor in some of those tunnels—old open graves and wide drains—rocks as sharp as needles that stuck out from the walls, and caves so fragile they rained great lumps of stone on whoever disturbed them. She could hear Gail behind her, and she knew he had no idea where he was going either until he remembered the matches in his pockets.

Another moment of light. He was alone with her, clutching the box of matches. For a brief second Sophie saw everything around her, and it burned itself onto her retinas like a photograph: three tunnels, a man-size crack in the floor, and a cluster of wetbugs hanging from the ceiling. And there, on the wall, a great whorl of silver, a scrubbed-out, glowing mess. Someone had destroyed the glowfish arrows, their directions back to the house.

Gail saw it, too.

"What have you done?" he hissed, then the match burned out and Sophie ran again. This time she knew where she was going, a fragment of memory pushing her legs toward the middle tunnel. She jumped over the crack in the floor, aimed for the space where the tunnel should have been, and entered another realm of darkness.

The floor was angled up. She spread her arms like wings to feel her way through, and this time she didn't hit anything. She ran and ran, and then she was in the chamber with the coffee machine, then out and by the stairs to the house, Ralf and Gail lost, howling in the catacombs behind her.

Chapter 26

Ralf and Gail, Gail and Ralf

All the house was quiet. The front door was still open but Cartwright had disappeared. Manic was still pegged down outside, where he pounded the ground with his dinner-plate hooves and snorted through his huge, steam-engine nose. Sophie approached slowly, her lungs and throat aching with exhaustion. The goose pimples on her arm were only just starting to go down.

"Where is he?" she asked softly. "Have you seen him, boy?"

The sea answered her with a low, grating wail and a band of dark clouds bottled up on the horizon. She patted Manic on the head.

"I'm going to find him," she said. "Don't you worry. We'll be out of here soon."

Manic looked distinctly unconvinced, but she went

inside anyway and trod softly up the stairs. The silence was disturbing. She had a horrible vision of Cartwright dead on the floor, and the Battleship swooping down on his body like a huge and insatiable vampire. Even though she knew they weren't in there, she tiptoed past the twins' room with the portrait of the horse, and nearly jumped when she caught its eye through the crack in the door.

She thought she was alone, combing corridor after corridor until she got lost and had to turn back. For an endless five minutes she walked in circles, and at some point she felt another presence behind her like it had crept out of the walls. When she got back to the twins' room the floor creaked. Her fingers twitched as she forced herself not to look back, but she quickened her pace as she walked into a moldy, white-paneled drawing room with a doorway at either end. Someone sneezed behind her, and she stopped.

"I'm sick of chasing you," Gail said bitterly. "I don't see the *point*."

"Then stop," she said. She leaned against the wall, drained, and looked at him. He was out of breath and covered in slime.

"Can't," he said.

"How long are you going to follow me?"

"I don't know," he said. His hair was sticking out at all

angles, unbrushed and sad looking. "But I wish you'd stop talking to me like that."

"Like what?" she said despairingly.

"In that reasonable voice. Like you're nice. You're only trying to get away from me."

"Of course I want to get away," she said. "What do you expect?"

"Ralf wants me to finish you off," he said. "Ralf says I should pick you up and carry you over to the window and throw you out. You've caused so much trouble, and it isn't fun anymore."

"That's what Ralf says," she replied, leaning away from him. "But what do *you* think? Do you want to throw me out of a window?"

Gail took something small and sharp from his pocket: a letter knife with a bone handle and Laurel's initials carved in it. His hand was shaking.

"I think he's right."

He moved toward her and she stepped back, raising her hands.

"You don't," she said. "I can see it every time you're together. You only do what he says because he's louder than you, and a bit taller, and a little bit older. But it doesn't mean he's in charge."

They moved across the room until he had her backed against a toothpaste-striped settee.

"What are you saying?" he asked, raising the letter knife to her eyes. Sophie tried to push the sofa out of the way, but it was nailed to the floor.

"I'm saying you could let me go," she said. "You don't have to hurt me, which I *know* you don't want to do, because underneath you're actually all right. Ralf would never have to know. He might not even come back, if something got him down there. You could let me walk away right now, and we'd both be happy."

Gail stared at her. She nodded, and he lowered the knife.

"You see?" she whispered. "Easy."

Gail hung his head. Then he snapped it up, laughing, and twirled the knife around in his fingers. He rolled his shoulders back, his spine cracking.

"That was fun," he said. "If this were a story, it would *definitely* have worked."

"What?" Sophie said, her heart jumping nervously. He stepped toward her and she fell into the sofa, which engulfed her like a wet sponge. "Gail?"

"Not Gail," he said. "Ralf this time. Ralf all the time, actually."

The floor creaked, and in the doorway they'd just

come through Ralf appeared again, seaweed dripping from his hair. He looked green, like he'd just recovered from a scare.

"That was a good trick, Silverfish," he said, spitting out a piece of slime. "What was it? A machine? A hologram? You've been learning from us."

"Ralf?" she said.

"That's not Ralf," said Gail.

"Not fair," said Ralf, stepping into the room. "You can't just change your mind like that."

"What are you talking about?" Sophie snapped. They looked at her with something like irritation, then they smiled beautifully like the sun had risen over their faces.

"I love it when we do this part," said Gail. "It's when I feel most clever."

"Poor Silverfish," said Ralf, wandering over. "You had no idea, did you? Not even Cartwright has worked it out, although he gets suspicious sometimes. This is our greatest performance, and we've been doing it all for you."

"Explain," she said, trying to stand up. She got her feet on the floor, but the twins were so close she was bending almost backward over the sofa.

"Bit slow, aren't you?" said Ralf.

"And you thought we were terrible actors," said Gail.

"The fact is, we're really quite brilliant. Even our *mother* is confused."

"Sometimes I wish someone would work it out, just once," said Ralf. "I mean, I'm starting to feel like everyone around us is an idiot. Nobody appreciates the effort we put in."

"But that's the curse of being a good actor."

"We're so good nobody ever applauds."

"Stop gloating," Sophie said, putting her hand to the cold metal under her sleeve. "I swear to Neptune, I don't have any more patience."

"I do so like it when the servant appeals to Gail to save them," said Gail, a hideous facsimile of his brother. "Go for the village idiot, they think. Save him from his terrible brother."

"As if it ever works," said Ralf.

"I suppose we're doing them a favor," added Gail. "I don't want them to die believing in goodness."

"Who are you?" Sophie said, desperate to keep them talking. The twins looked annoyed by her interjection.

"Oh, right," said was-Gail. "We don't know."

"We were definitely *born* Ralf and Gail," said was-Ralf, "but we spent so long swapping we got confused. Now we just take turns. Good, isn't it?"

"It passes the time," said was-Gail.

"Well, it's been fun, Silverfish," said was-Ralf. "Sorry. We're going to have to get rid of you now."

Sophie scrambled over the back of the sofa and used it as a barricade. They let her try, then moved toward her slowly, each stepping around a side of the sofa with incredibly bored expressions.

"Is this always your plan?" she said. "A grand reveal?"

"Yes," they both said at once, then scowled at each other.

"We have to give you some credit," continued was-Gail. "You're the only one who's worked out where the box was. And getting out of the clock room—not many have done that, either."

"Must be why Cartwright likes you."

Sophie tripped backward over a chair, and they sniggered in unison.

"You killed the other Bone Snatchers," she said as she scrambled back up.

"They died falling through the clock room or going through rotten floorboards. Getting trapped in locked rooms. Some of them really did vanish in the night, but I don't fancy their chances much," said was-Ralf.

"You should have seen Cartwright's face every time we polished one off," said was-Gail.

"It was tragic. He so wanted to believe they'd run away. He's soft on the inside."

"We faked some notes. It kept Mother off our backs, too."

"Amazing how a piece of paper can allay guilt."

"Scree, though—that's an interesting one."

Sophie grabbed a poker from the fireplace and swung it in front of her. The twin who had been Ralf caught it in his fist, and was-Gail bent it in half.

"Tell me about Scree!" she blurted. If only she could *think*.

"Right," was-Ralf said. "Well, after he started *chatting* to you and letting you go to the clock room, we were worried he might ruin everything. So we had a word with him, and when that wasn't enough, we taught him a lesson or two. Jumping out at him at night, stalking him through the catacombs, that kind of thing. Turns out he wasn't as tough as we thought."

"It only took a day for him to lose it. He threw himself into the sea, didn't he?"

"Wish we could have been there to see it. But he left a note of his own. Ironic, in a way."

Was-Gail drew something from his pocket and waved it in Sophie's face. There was no mistaking Scree's messy scribble, and she could tell from the twins' faces that they hadn't forged it. They looked positively disappointed.

"What shall we do with her?" said was-Ralf.

"Lock her in a cupboard?"

"Too slow. She'll get out before she starves."

"You're not going to win, Gail," Sophie said. "No matter how hard you try. The game's won."

"I'm Ralf," was-Gail said, baring his teeth. "I told you."

"That's not fair," said was-Ralf to him. "You're still Gail. Chop chop, fall to my heel."

"I am *clearly* Ralf, you cretin."

"It's not your turn."

"I was Ralf first!"

"*I* was Ralf first!"

Sophie whipped the scissors from her sleeve, only to have them snatched away.

"Look at that," said was-Gail, holding them aloft. "She thought she could slip away while we were arguing. What an unoriginal idea."

"Another thing that never really works. Does she think we're stupid?"

"You think she would have learned by now."

"I think, it being a special occasion, that we can both be Ralf today."

Sophie looked from one twin to the other. They had backed her into a corner, and now they weren't moving, only leaning forward at the hips as though inspecting her through monocles.

"In the sea?" asked Ralf.

"In the sea," said Ralf.

In a blur of anger, Sophie did two things that seemed to happen at once: she ground her heel into the foot of Ralf on the right, who screamed, and drove her elbow into the other Ralf's crotch. He dropped the scissors, which she grabbed as his fists swung over her head.

"That's for Scree!" she screamed, and lashed out with the open scissors as the twins fell upon her.

At first she didn't think she'd hit either of them, but they both leaped back, astonished, one of them clutching his scarlet hand. The bloodied Ralf opened his mouth, but no sound came out.

"She took the end off your finger," his brother said, as though it wasn't obvious. "She cut it off!"

Only the very tip of his index finger had been sliced off, but the bright red color transfixed the twins for second. Sophie bolted, shoving through them and running back into the corridor.

"She took my finger," Ralf moaned, sounding momentarily like Gail, but then his voice twisted and changed: "Get her!" he screamed. "Twist her head off!"

"Come on, then!" she screamed back, plunging down the stairs and skidding into the entrance hall, where the door was wide open and Manic was pulling at his peg. "Come and get me, you freaks!"

As she swerved toward the door she heard a terrible scream coming from upstairs, like Cartwright had just had his own fingers twisted off, and he rushed down, clutching the Monster Box in his arms. It leered at them with its twisted keyhole eye. The Battleship was after him, and in her fist she held a clump of his hair.

"Lock them in!" Cartwright yelled to Sophie, and she ran through the door before him. They started heaving the doors shut, but the Battleship's huge hand shot through and grabbed the edge of the frame, forcing it back open. They both slammed their bodies against the door and pushed back.

"I've got to tell you something about your uncle," she gasped, remembering the room of gold.

"Right now?" Cartwright shouted through the commotion. "Is this *really* the time?"

"Sure, let's do it over a nice cup of tea!" she said as the Battleship's fingers slithered around, looking for a hold.

"It's no use," said Cartwright. "We're not going to get away in time."

"We are," said Sophie. "You can outrun her on Manic. Make her chase you through the gardens. The twins are after me because I cut their finger off—"

"What?"

"—but I don't think they know you have the box yet."

"How are you going to escape those maniacs?"

In her pocket, Scree's watch began to tick and vibrate. Despite everything, Sophie felt a grin of triumph twitch the corners of her mouth. It was nearly lunchtime.

"I'm going to take them onto the rocks and get rid of them," she said. "I'm going to give the monsters the best meal of their lives."

"I think there's a good chance you're going to—" they both slammed their bodies against the door as it moved an inch "—die a horrible death!"

"You haven't seen me angry," she said. "One—"

"Two—"

"Three!"

They let go of the door and sprang to the sides. Cartwright ran after Manic, who reared and tore the peg out of the ground. The Battleship and the twins fell through the door, the bloodied Ralf an interesting shade of screaming purple. As Cartwright scrambled onto Manic and tore through the gardens, the Monster Box under his arm, Sophie took off in the direction of the sea.

The twins ran after her, hands outstretched, gaining on her with every step as they moved toward the razor-sharp, pointed rocks that leered out of the waves.

Chapter 27

A Monster's Call

As Sophie pounded toward the sea it felt like the distance in front of her was growing, the island unraveling like a long tentacle, and that she would never reach the water's edge. She thought her body was going to seize up. She'd never been good at cross-country in school, and by now she must have outstripped even the most tenacious runner. Her breath was hot and ragged and her feet were like blocks of burning lead. But still she ran.

The twins were behind her, sounding equally winded. Was-Ralf, whose finger she'd sliced off, had managed to stanch it with the cloth from his shirt, and was trundling toward her with the determination of a machine. They'd started bickering again, shooting single words at each other like snipers.

She struggled to the edge of the island, where the garden melted into the sea and the rocks rose like cragged teeth. She didn't know yet how she was going to defend herself from the sea creatures, which were looking at her like a tasty, fleshy sandwich—she'd forgotten about the morning feeding, hadn't she?—or how she'd get them to take both of the twins. But there was nowhere else to go, and she hardly cared what happened anymore, now there was no New Continent and no parents to prove herself to. Even the stories she had were stuttering through her head like fallen soldiers.

"Silverfish," gasped the twins. "Come to us, pretty Silverfish."

Sophie entered the water. She knew the creatures loved blood, but was-Ralf had raised his injured hand over his head, perhaps knowing that it would bring the monsters toward him like flies to rotten fruit. She waded through the shallows and climbed onto a large stone, flat like a molar and surrounded by long incisors.

"Give us a kiss before you die, Silverfish," was-Gail sang, and they both found it so funny they struck up a tune. "Give us a kiss, Silverfish. Give us a kiss, Silverfish." They chanted it over and over, lower and lower, until it was almost a hum. "Give us a kiss, Silverfish . . ."

The tide was low, and Sophie could see in the rocks

surrounding her hundreds of holes that led to the catacombs. The air was static with unbroken lightning, the sky ready to fall down on them at any moment. She considered scrambling down one of the holes, but they were dangerously narrow and lined with razor clams.

The twins entered the water, looking a lot happier now they didn't have to run. They picked their way through the rocks as Sophie climbed farther into the sea, her foot- and handholds becoming smaller and more precarious with every step.

"Give us a kiss, Silverfish!" they sang, and made horrible slurping noises like they were about to swallow her.

Loose pieces of rock splashed into the water by Sophie's feet. The sea creatures rose from the breaking surf, opening their mouths and displaying their teeth. She saw Cartwright galloping over the long curve of the island, the Monster Box held aloft, and behind him a trail of flattened plants and trees, the Battleship plowing through them like a duck through water. Cartwright wouldn't get back in time to help fight off the twins and the monsters. She was on her own.

With the scissors still clutched in her hand, she opened them up and made a quick cut along her index finger. A long, red line opened up and pearls of blood appeared.

She bent down and plunged her hand into the water. The creatures chattered excitedly among themselves in clicks and whispers and whistles.

"Do you give up *now*?" said was-Gail as they got close to her. They pulled themselves out of the water and faced her on a long, flat rock. With a quick glance at each other they reached into their jackets and withdrew knives.

"You must be tired," added was-Gail, twirling his around.

"They never are," said was-Ralf, looking at her with pure hatred as his finger continued to seep. "They punch and fight and shout and beg, but no matter how long they string it out, they never win."

Sophie held the scissors, stained and bent out of shape, in front of her like a dagger. The water below her seethed, and a barbed tentacle shot up and grabbed them out of her hand. There was a *crunch* as the bloodstained scissors were chewed up.

"Oh," she said, blinking at her empty hand.

"Oh indeed," was-Ralf said, looking delighted. "Anything you want to say?"

"You still don't have to do this," she said.

"Don't try that again," said was-Gail. He dodged forward, fingers outstretched, and jabbed her in the side so hard she doubled over.

As she clutched her stomach she saw the water. The creatures were shifting and getting agitated, but the twins were too focused on Sophie to care.

Next to her chest, pressed between her grubby shirt and her skin, Mister Scree's pocket watch began to sing.

"It doesn't matter what you do to me," she said. "Cartwright already has the Monster Box. We're going to cure Sea Fever."

"That's what you think it does?" said was-Ralf.

"Interesting," said was-Gail.

The twins, as one, smirked. They strode over to her, one-two-three, and as their blades sailed toward her chest something broke the water behind them and a huge, purplish tentacle whipped through the air. The twins screamed as they were caught by the monster. Sophie dodged backward in a cold panic, stepping right off the rock. There was a moment of falling, so surprising that she didn't have time to cry out. Instead of feeling her body skewered by the rocks, though, something fleshy but hard slammed into Sophie's back and she was thrown into the air.

In a half-second glance she saw the twins being constricted by the demikraken, wailing and stabbing uselessly at the tree-trunk-thick tentacle around their waists. Then she was caught by a giant squid, which suckered itself to her flesh and pulled her down into the sea.

She plunged into blinding coldness. She felt the weight of the sea above her like a huge black rock, and as colored lights exploded behind her eyes she wondered at the point of trying to survive when there was nothing good to run to. Something wrapped itself around her boots and started pulling them off. They were going to peel her like a banana before eating her.

As she drifted away it felt like there were streamers tightening around her foot. Even here, close to drowning, it felt familiar. More creatures crowded around her, making quick jabs at her, testing how tender she was. The streamers curled themselves around her toes, and she kicked weakly. The thing tightened on her sixth toe. *What a place to start eating from*, she thought vaguely. *Just before it ends, I'll have ten toes like everybody else.*

The thing on her feet went rigid, and there was a high-pitched cry like a train braking underwater. Sophie felt herself moving through the water, although she couldn't tell whether she was going up or down or to the side. Was it going to dash her against a rock? But then she broke the surface, and the tentacle gripping her raised her so high she could see everything: the house and its garden, the twins still punching and kicking with the thing that had them, and Cartwright trying to push the Battleship into the water. Her first lungful of air was so painful she cried out, and the next was so good tears streamed down her face. The thing that had made the noise, the thing on her foot, was still attached, and she looked down to see it: a pale octopus with a head the size of a golf ball. And she remembered. It was bigger now, but without a doubt it was the thing she'd found in the rock pool after she'd escaped the Room of Remains. Its cry spread through the sea, repeated and echoed by dozens, then hundreds of the creatures, a secret message bouncing among them and all around the island. The tentacle holding her aloft brought her down and slowly, almost gently, placed her back on the rock.

It let go. The octopus plopped back into the water. Sophie scrambled to the side of the rock and tried to catch sight of it, but it disappeared in a jet of bubbles.

"Come back!" she yelled, although she didn't know why, or what good it would do. She wheezed, coughing up seawater. "You paid me back."

"Silverfish," gasped was-Ralf, making her turn around. "Get this thing off us!"

The twins were still on the rock, each turning an unusual shade as they were slowly squeezed. They'd both dropped their knives.

"Not until you call me by my real name," she said.

"Slitherfish!" howled was-Gail, and she turned away, squeezing her eyes shut. But she could stand the sound of their strangulation even less than the sight.

Then the high-pitched cry echoed through the water one more time, louder than before, and the tentacle around the twins, instead of crushing them tighter—instead of finishing them—withdrew before she could make a decision.

They fell to the ground, gasping, and stared at her with terrified eyes. For a moment she had no idea what to do.

"I did that," she said. The lie tripped out of her mouth as easily as a story. "The creatures know I look after them, so they let me go. And they let you go, too, because I told them to."

"You saved us?" said was-Gail. He looked like he couldn't believe what had happened. "You called them off?"

Her mind raced. *The creatures thought the twins are my friends.*

"Yes," she said quickly. "But not because you aren't evil. It's because I'm better than you."

"But . . ." said was-Gail. He looked at his brother, who

was clutching his hand and still hadn't spoken. "What do we do now?"

"You go back to the island and stay there," said Sophie. "You tell your mother to stop hurling herself after us, and you let me and Cartwright leave. In return, I won't set the creatures on you."

"Liar," said was-Ralf quietly. They both turned toward him, confused. He looked at his bandaged hand, the red soaking through. "Liar!" he repeated, and grabbed his knife, which had clattered to the floor, and his brother, without thinking, did the same, and they scrambled to-ward her blade-first.

"Get them!" she screamed at the sea, but she knew the creatures didn't really understand, and they only poked their tentacles out of the water like they were acknowledg-ing her thanks. "GET THEM!" she screamed again, and as she ducked to the side the first blade missed her com-pletely but the second only missed its real target, her chest, and she was stabbed in the shoulder.

The wound wasn't deep, but it was painful, and she nearly vomited. The twins circled her, eyes wide with glee. She couldn't believe it. She couldn't believe that, after everything, they'd actually *won*.

And then something moved behind them.

"My boys," said a creaky voice. The twins turned, knives still raised. Sophie, clutching her shoulder, thought she must be hallucinating from pain or exhaustion, but the twins could see it, too, she knew they could, because they were completely still. An old man, thin and battered as a skeleton, was rising from the sea, water streaming off his gray robes, holding something in his hand that could be—must be—a scythe. He almost looked like—

"Laurel?" Sophie whispered.

"Father?" said was-Gail.

"But you're dead," said was-Ralf stupidly.

"I was," said the Thing, pushing back its cowl to reveal his hollow cheeks and a wide, yellow-toothed grin. "You would know, because you killed me. But Neptune spat me back out so I could see you one last time."

He moved toward the twins with his crooked fingers outstretched, and just for a second, the tiniest fraction of a moment, he looked at Sophie and winked. And she knew what she was meant to do. Before the twins could react she barreled into them with all her strength, and was-Ralf fell sideways, scrambled for a handhold, and slipped into the sea. His brother shrieked and tried to stab her again with his knife, but she grabbed his wrist, twisting the weapon out of his grasp and pushing him down after his brother.

They both missed the sharp rocks, but the creatures were still there and, seeing Sophie throw them down, needed no further excuse to attack.

There was a huge, black, bubbling mess as tentacles and teeth and claws fought for the twins, and then they all sank under the water, and there was nothing left but a little shred of bloodied bandage, turning over and over on the surface.

Chapter 28

The Monster Box

Laurel, newly raised from the dead, regarded Sophie with something like approval. She stepped toward him, mesmerized, and reached out to touch him. He shook his head, then did something completely un-ghostlike and coughed up a piece of seaweed.

"Well?" he said in a voice she knew only too well. "Nothing to say?"

The pain in her shoulder was radiating through her chest, and there were purple spots floating in front of her eyes, but Sophie cleared her head for long enough to see what was really in front of her. The ghost's scythe wasn't a scythe but a chewed-up fishing contraption; he wasn't wearing the robes of the Grim Reaper, but his own torn and tattered clothing, gray and slimy after days of living underground.

"I found your *teeth!*" she spluttered.

"So?" said Mister Scree. "You think I don't have spares? The creachers have a set off me every month."

He reached out to steady her as she swayed forward, clutching her shoulder.

"How long were you down there?" she asked.

"Long enough. I took sandwiches."

"You scrubbed the directions off the walls. . . ."

"Didn't want the twins catching you," he said, his face settling in a well-practiced grimace.

"It almost sounds like you care," she said, smiling.

"I don't care about anyone," he grumbled. "I'm too old for all that. The twins were getting too nasty, and I knew it'd all end in tears, and look, I was right—scissors and knives and blood everywhere! So I practiced being dead. Thought they'd get bored and I could come back when it was safe."

"You stopped them from killing me," she said. She wanted to add more, but Scree was frowning with something like embarrassment. "Thank you," Sophie said somberly.

He grunted, flushing pink, and gestured for her to follow. They picked their way toward the shore, the old man and the bleeding girl, back to the house on the hill and the huge, deserted gardens.

"Got something you ought to know," Scree told her as they waded through the shallows. The creatures remained at a safe distance, watching carefully but satisfied for the moment by the twins. "It's no excuse, but I should've told you what happened to all the servants. I wasn't sure at first, but I reckon I was lying to myself when I didn't realize they were dying. Didn't think any son of his lordship's could be so bad as to murder people."

"You warned me not to get involved," she said. "You couldn't stop me. And now it's almost over. We're going to open the Monster Box and see what's inside."

Scree nodded, and she thought she saw a tear roll down his cheek. Her hand reached for his.

"You loved him, didn't you," she said. "Laurel, I mean."

"Call it what you will," he said, jerking his fingers away, but only after a second. "Her Battleshipness thought it was monstrous. She hated me and she hated him, but I stayed with him through thick and thin, even when he was moonstruck. And I stayed here after and looked after 'em all, 'cause I thought I owed it to 'em, even though they made this place miserable. I thought the best I could do was keep my nose out of their business, catch fish, and keep serving dinner. Those that were alive wanted to keep the box hidden, and him that was . . . *dead* . . . wanted young Cartwright to have it. How could I do everything right at once?"

"You couldn't," she said. "I'm sorry. But you couldn't."

"Aye," he said as they reached the shore. "But now your young man has the Monster Box, the twins are fish food, and Laurel got his way."

"Cartwright's not my—"

"'Course not," he said craftily.

They climbed through the garden, the storm gathering at their backs like a pulled seam, the sea darkly chopped up and grumbling.

"What do you think's in it?" said Mister Scree. "You two seem pretty keen on getting it open."

"It's a cure for Sea Fever," she said. "Or we think it is. But just now the twins seemed to think it was something different. I don't know if I *want* to open the box."

"Maybe you should do it anyway," said Mister Scree, leaning on his fishing contraption. "Maybe it's time to let the story run its course."

A loud whinnying bent around the corner of the island, and Manic blasted into view, clumps of earth scattering under his feet. Cartwright was clinging on for dear life, his clothes and hair in disarray, the Monster Box wedged under his arm. They slid to a halt in front of the house and he dropped the box, which despite its lightness buried itself in the earth with a *thump*.

"What's wrong?" Sophie asked as Cartwright slid off, landing in a pile on the floor. "She's not *still* chasing you, is she?"

Manic reared and thundered off by himself before Sophie could grab the reins.

"She's mad, too," Cartwright gasped. "She's phenomenally, unspeakably *insane*. She bit Manic! Like he was a steak! And I thought you were bad."

He saw Scree and stopped dead. Sophie was about to explain, but then the Battleship arrived, bursting out of the foliage, thistles gripped in each hand. Even Scree backed away, but Sophie was too busy staring to notice that Cartwright had also dodged and left the path between her and the Battleship clear.

The Battleship obviously didn't care who she got her hands on, only that she got them on someone. Everyone was her enemy now. She didn't bat an eyelid when she passed Scree, whose absence she might even have forgotten.

"I want all of you off my island!" she shouted, advancing like a tank. "It's gone on for too long! I've put up with too much, and you're not going to take it away from me now."

She glided over to Sophie, raising her hand to deliver a stinging slap across the face, then stopped and wavered. Two fat tears rolled down her cheeks, and her small mouth opened to deliver not a war cry but a small, hopeless sob.

"Are they dead?" she asked. Sophie nodded. The Battleship sat down, her skirts sweeping to the sides like a gray mushroom. Suddenly she looked more human, her hair and clothes washed-out, her body shrinking into itself like a punctured balloon.

Sophie sat down in front of the Battleship so the top of her head was level with the woman's chin.

"I'm sorry," she said, because she knew that's what you're meant to say. "I didn't mean for them to die."

The Battleship's face scrunched up like a great handkerchief until it looked like it was going to swallow itself, then it flattened, leaving her tear-stained and red.

"Disgusting magpie," she said.

"It's over," said Sophie. "We've got the Monster Box, and it's us three against you. You just have to let it go."

"Little slug," the Battleship growled, and halfheartedly swiped at Sophie, who stepped backward to avoid the blow. The bleeding in her shoulder had almost stopped, leaving a large, crusted patch of red on her shirt.

She didn't know why she was being nice to the mother

of those monsters. She thought the Battleship was weak, and nasty, and was probably a terrible parent as well. But what did she know? How could she imagine what it was like to be under the thumbs of your children, or to have created your own personal hell?

She dug the golden tickets out of her pocket where she had stuffed them earlier, now wet and clumped together. She threw them down at Cartwright's feet, and it took a moment for him to understand what they were.

"Your uncle made these," she said shortly. "There are thousands of them in the house. He lied to you. He lied to everyone. He sent thousands of people to their deaths. My parents, too."

"I don't under—"

"The New Continent isn't real. He made it up, Cartwright, and sold it to you and everyone else, posters and all, and now everyone's at the bottom of the sea. The Sea Fever meant everyone was mad enough to believe him."

Cartwright looked, for a moment, as though he might draw his sword and hit her for being so blasphemous. But then he deflated. He knew she was telling the truth.

"He would have told me," he said halfheartedly.

"He was going to, I think. But he died before he had

the chance. He didn't think the end would come so soon. Probably the twins pushed him into the water."

A strange thing happened then: she realized that everyone was looking at her, waiting to see what she would do next. Even the Battleship had quelled her sobs and was looking up like a child waiting for a story.

She didn't know what to do. She'd seen the twins die, watched Scree rise from the dead, and experienced the Battleship crumbling like a fortress made of biscuits. She was tired. She wanted everything to be over.

"Aren't you going to open the box?" she said to Cartwright.

Cartwright untied the key from his neck. In this light its bronze tentacles seemed to dance and writhe, made worse by the fog in her head. He started to bend down, then stopped and tossed the key away from him. For a moment it glinted at the top of its arc; then it fell down, down, and down, and landed at Sophie's feet.

"It's yours," he said. "You deserve it."

So Sophie went to the box, and she opened it.

Chapter 29

The Last Meal

The top of the box slid up and back on a delicate, complicated system of weights and levers. Inside was a small, gold horn attached to a glass music box, and inside the glass music box were wheels and saws and strings. Something began to turn, winding a silver thread tight around a spiked bobbin. A piece of yellowing paper stuck to the inside of the box flapped in the breeze, and Sophie read it before it skidded away.

Laurel's Patent Monster Box
The world's first Creature Caller.
May the ones who open this box be forever damned!
~ Double bluffs a specialty ~

"Oh, Neptune," said Sophie.

The box began to wheeze. And the creatures stirred.

***

The Battleship hiccupped as Sophie tried to slam the box shut, but it had latched itself open.

At first there was only a whine, like the mechanism was broken, but then it started rising so fast that within seconds it was a scream. And still it kept going, past the point of any noise she had heard before, so loud it felt like her eardrums were going to burst. She threw it away from her and the noise wavered, pulsing like an emergency siren. Out at sea a long, nasal moan joined the noise and shook the foundations of the house.

"What's happening?" shouted Cartwright, stuffing his fingers in his ears. Sophie looked at Scree, but he was as surprised as her, tightly clutching his fishing pole.

"What's wrong?" Cartwright yelled. "Is it meant to be doing this?"

She stumbled to him. Another moan rose from the sea, a sound like the kraken and all its friends having their teeth extracted. They rose and began to surge toward the shore. Not just the creatures that usually loitered around the island: they were coming from farther away, too, the horizon bending as the sea heaved itself up to vomit forth all its creatures.

She grabbed Cartwright's sleeve and yanked him away

from the Monster Box. They plunged into the twisting greenery of the overgrown garden.

When they could just about hear each other she grasped his collar.

"We're in trouble," she said.

"Why?"

"The twins knew there was something bad in the Monster Box, but I didn't listen!"

"What is it?" he shouted. The expression on his face was one of dawning horror.

"I saw some of Laurel's diagrams in the Room of Remains. That shrieking from the box—it attracts the creatures, it riles them up and sends them into a feeding frenzy, but there aren't any bones left for them. They'll tear everything down, and then they're going to smash us to pieces. We're the last meal!"

"You're wrong," he yelled through the siren and the screams of the approaching monsters. "My uncle wouldn't give me something that could kill me!"

Even now, she wanted to shake him for being so thick.

"He only pretended to give it to you!"

"I was there when he said—"

"He knew what the twins were like," she said. The first monsters were beginning to squirm up the banks. "That's why he said he was leaving the Monster Box to you. He knew they'd get jealous and steal it—it was probably the only way he could get them to take it without them getting suspicious. He left the box in his workroom, right in the middle of the floor so they would find it, with the key so they could open it. Except they missed the key, and *you* found it, and it gave them enough time to work out what the box really was."

"But to *have us eaten*—"

"He knew you'd leave the island after they stole the box. He didn't know you'd keep coming back for it. Even if you did come back, you should have found nothing but a pile of rubble. But the twins realized it was dangerous. They haven't just been taunting you, they've been trying to keep their freakish little world intact. The cure Laurel talked about wasn't for Sea Fever. It was for this horrible place."

A tentacle slapped down on the ground beside them. Sophie dodged, and together they stumbled deeper into the garden, away from the oncoming army. Cartwright kept his head turned from her, and she knew it was so she couldn't see his expression.

When they stopped, Cartwright finally looked at her. His face dropped.

"You stupid, obsessive idiot," Sophie said. "It's because

you wouldn't let go of the box. What are we meant to do now?"

Cartwright looked at her. Sophie found herself leaning in, and so was he, and they kissed, briefly, on the mouth. As soon as she thought the word *finally* she realized she'd been waiting for it for a long time, even though Cartwright made her want to punch a wall, even though he was a coward and a liar and a total idiot. Although she wasn't so great either, charging around and stabbing innocent people with scissors.

Maybe he wasn't that bad, in comparison.

She pulled away, her stomach twisting itself into surprised but not unpleasant knots and said, "Gross."

"Too soon?"

They heard the thudding of hooves. The chopping of gravestone teeth.

"I meant what do we *do*? Now?"

"I think our escape vehicle has arrived," said Cartwright.

They fought their way out of the undergrowth to see a wall of creatures rising out of the sea, advancing along the shore in an army, and there, thrashing madly in front of them, with a rubbery tentacle hanging out of his mouth like a piece of spaghetti, was Manic.

They looked at each other.

"It's better than nothing," Sophie suggested, and they ran toward him.

Cartwright swung himself onto Manic's back as the first wave of creatures came down. The squid were knotted together in impossible shapes, caught up in the surge and thrown to shore still writhing, and behind them loomed one of the most monstrous creatures of the sea, the huge black demikraken with circles of teeth gleaming in its open mouth. The creatures hit the shore, bringing with them a sheet of salt water, and surged toward the shrieking Monster Box. A brown crab emerged from the fray and ran toward it, but was snatched back by something with too many legs.

They brought with them the stench of seaweed and dredged sewers. Sophie gagged as Cartwright hauled her up after him. Manic gnashed his teeth and took a chunk out of a wobbling jellyfish which had decided to wrap itself around his head.

"Away from the house," Sophie called over the deafening scream, and Cartwright urged Manic forward. Sophie had hoped they'd be able to leap over the sea as Cartwright had done on his arrival, but the sky had been almost blocked out by the creatures and they would only be throwing themselves into a mouth.

"STOP!" she screamed at them, but her voice was lost in the chomping and gnashing. They didn't even seem to recognize her and surged past with snapping jaws. Cartwright tried to gallop ahead of the creatures, but they were everywhere, and now that the first wave had arrived other things were heaving themselves out of the water: something gray from the bottom of the ocean that looked like a giant tapeworm, an ancient dragonfish, a barnacled griddle pan that had awoken from a decades-long sleep. An eel slapped down in front of them so they had to turn back. A tentacle went through a window in the house, spraying the ground with glass, and all hell that had not already happened broke loose.

There were hundreds of them. Thousands even, she realized, more than she'd ever thought possible in all the world. The sea was thick with them and their viscous, blackish blood as they fought amongst themselves to get to the shore. Chunks of masonry fell off the side of the house, and soon things were climbing up it, suckering themselves to the damp stone and crushing roof tiles under their feelers. Despite herself, Sophie couldn't help but watch as the front of the house was torn off, first the lower floors, then the top slipping after it like warm butter. The innards of the house were spread out, upholstery being sucked off moldering armchairs like loose skin from a plum, paintings snapped up like bits of cereal, suits of armor thrown around between the creatures until something with teeth like an industrial disposal unit managed to crush them up.

Manic was struggling through knee-deep slime and blubber. None of the monsters were interested in them yet, but it was only a matter of time before they were caught in the fight and eaten themselves.

"This way!" Cartwright shouted, or she thought he shouted, because she was almost deaf from the noise. He tried to steer them toward the back of the house, but she knew that it was useless. There were creatures around the other side already, still coming fast, trampling the remains of the oyster racks, and if they weren't eaten they'd be crushed by the falling house. She looked around wildly for Scree and the Battleship. Scree was balanced precariously on a tall stack of rock, beating tentacles away with his fishing claw. The Battleship was still on the ground, batting things off with her elbows, and she had the Monster Box with her, which she was trying to bash to pieces with a brick. But the thing was indestructible, and she didn't even make a dent in it before she disappeared. Within seconds all Sophie could see of the Battleship was a puff of white skirt slowly being sucked into a mass of writhing flesh. She reached out, wanting to pull her back out, but she was too far away. Her hand closed on air and the Battleship was lost.

She could see right inside the house now. Into the twins' junk room, and the dining room, and the clock room, the huge bell swinging under the weight of the attack. Manic was trampling monsters with decreasing effectiveness, and Cartwright had his sword out, swinging it wildly at anything that got too close. Sophie ducked her head and looked at the seething ground. The Monster Box bobbed to the surface, still screeching, and Sophie had an idea that would probably but not definitely get her killed. It was, she considered, better than nothing.

She jumped down from the horse and plunged toward the box.

The first thing Sophie did when she hit the ground was fall over. Everything was wet and covered in a sheet of slime, and the chaos around her was so all-consuming that her senses shut down and for a moment all she could see was blurred, moving shapes. The box was swamped by something fleshy, its noise descending into a low, strangled whine. The noise that she could hear over it was stomach-churning: slurping, chopping, sucking, and the sporadic ripping sound of curtains or carpet or *please no* skin. She searched for the box on her hands and knees, rolling to the side as a purple limb swept over her head. Cartwright, only just realizing that she wasn't behind him anymore, struggled to turn Manic around.

"What are you doing?" he shouted, or she thought he shouted as he skewered a stingray.

"I don't know," she said to herself, and managed to grab the open box as it was flung aside. The siren picked up again.

The house was a wreck. It rose on one side, only the far wall of the left wing completely intact, trailing down into half-chewed, shredded floors and furniture. The insides of the house had never been exposed to this much daylight, and they looked sad and broken and dead. The demikraken on her right sniffed the air, looking for a moment just like the Battleship, its huge nostrils flaring, and swooped down on her.

Whomp.

A thick tail fin flew over her head, its serrated edges glinting in the sun, just missing her scalp. Cartwright struggled over and swung his sword at it, severing the tip of the tail and prompting an anguished shriek.

"Don't do that," she said. "Don't hurt any of them!"

"Are you joking?" he yelled as a huge leech attempted to attach itself to his leg. "They're going to eat us!"

Sophie wedged the open box under her arm and began to climb through the fray, pushing her way through the fat tentacles and slippery entrails of creatures that had got in the way of something else's teeth. Her ears screamed for her to stop. She got to where the door used to be, narrowly avoiding a lump of falling ceiling, and entered into the carcass of the house. The main stairs reached into nowhere, but she took them anyway, and when they broke off she climbed along the beams sticking out of the exposed inner wall. They bent beneath her, and she suspected she had nothing to prevent her from falling but blind luck. Up one set of beams, along a tilting floor, and onto the next bits of wood which stuck out like pegs. Already she was dizzyingly high, and a tentacle tried to slap her away, so hard she almost dropped the box.

When she was as high as she could go she dropped onto the next floor, which was open to the air and leaned sharply to the side, and ran. Her foot went through the floor twice, and as she moved the whole structure groaned. The portraits and ornamental swords shook with the house. And then she was in the clock room, and she grasped a stone column and began to climb, toward the highest point she could get to. The box started to slide from under her arm. She wedged it between herself and the wall, scraping it against the stone, her foot continually slipping and knocking bits of plaster to the faraway ground, until she reached the top and pulled herself over.

Up here she could see and be seen by everything. She could see the shape of the storm on the horizon, which had arms and legs like a monster and crackled with hunger. It slowly spread toward them, feeling its way through the sky with its dark, ropy limbs, flashing and snapping as the creatures beneath it continued to feed.

The world looked very small, but she felt even smaller. The creatures slammed themselves against the wall she was balanced on, trying to knock her down into their mouths. She stumbled. Cartwright was down there, but she couldn't see the expression on his face, only that he was seconds away from being eaten.

"Hey!" she screamed. "Monsters! Look at me! Do you recognize me? I'm the Bone Snatcher!"

The creatures slammed against the wall again, and stones slipped from under her knees.

"You're mine!" she screamed. "You will not hurt anyone else on this island!"

She held the Monster Box aloft, gathering all her strength. Then she threw the box away from her and it fell, screeching that inhuman, painfully high sound. It did what she wanted; it got the creatures' attention, and for a moment they were all looking hungrily toward her. Then the box hit the ground below the bell and shattered.

The wailing cut off, leaving a huge gap in the air, a hole where the noise had been. The silence was horrendous. Sophie drew herself to her full height and opened her mouth to call off the creatures.

Then the demikraken, with a pained shriek, slammed its entire body against the column she was standing on.

Sophie dropped to her knees and yelped. The creatures, seeing the demikraken, screamed and went back to their meal, writhing and twisting through the ruins of the house. That wasn't meant to happen. *It was meant to break the frenzy. They were meant to snap out of it.*

Knees buckling, she looked down at the bell. It was almost the only thing left. How else were they going to recognize her, all of them at once, as the person who fed them and looked after them? She needed to knock them back to their senses. She needed to make them remember who she was so they'd let her go.

The demikraken slammed against the wall again. Something shifted below her and the wall began to lean, settling at a horrible angle. She pried a stone from under her feet, one as big as her head, and heaved it into her arms. Then she threw it down as hard as she could.

It fell into the depths of the bell's machinery, and for a second it looked like nothing would happen, that this was the end and she was about to be finished. Then there was movement—a cog knocked loose, a lever released. Something mechanical groaned, and there was the slow sliding of levers, and the pent-up, quickening spin of a hundred wheels.

The feeding bell was struck for the last time.

The sound of the bell, which the creatures had not heard in days, did something incredible to them. They fell down, blinking like fish pulled out of the water, exhausted by their frenzy. The monsters from farther afield, the ancient ones who had never heard the bell through their deep-sea slumber, crumpled up as though the noise hurt them and plopped back into the water, one by one.

The sheer size and weight of the bell, the deep, brassy sound that turned the air thick with shaking, dislodged its own foundations. Slowly, slowly, the struts it hung from bent. The bell was ripped from its chain and fell, landing with an almighty clang that cracked the rock beneath it.

For a moment Sophie was still in the air, looking down. The fuzz in her head from the Monster Box and the bell, from injury and exhaustion, made her wonder how real everything was. But there, on the ground and piled up the sides of the building, her creatures were stretching toward her, opening their mouths and howling with something that sounded like delight.

She heard Scree's voice drift up through the ruins, thin and proud:

"She's bloody gone and done it. She's got them under her thumb. They'll make her their queen!"

And then the wall she was on slipped forward, and Sophie fell.

Chapter 30

The Crowning

Sophie Seacove might have been dead.

She wasn't sure, but it was a distinct possibility. Everything was black, and heavy, and smelled of fish. She hoped the afterlife didn't always smell of fish. Unless the sea creatures had followed her here, in which case she would put up with anything.

She remembered the looks on their faces as she fell, if they could be called *looks* at all. They were very happy to see her. It wasn't their fault that the sound of the Monster Box had driven them mad; it tapped into some faulty wiring that made them into crazed animals, just like a few carefully placed words could make Sophie turn her fists on someone or cause water to leak out of her eyes. Water was leaking out of her eyes now, in fact, joining with the sea.

She grimaced, and in that moment realized that she had a mouth, and that it still moved even though she was dead. She moved her fingers and became instantly aware of small parts of her body, her cheek and her elbows, all of the bits pressed against the ground. Because there was a ground, and it was sharp and gravelly.

This was not what the afterlife was supposed to be like.

She opened her eyes. She was on the shore of Catacomb Hill, right by the water. She was surrounded by bits of rubble. The water was slapping against itself, but there were other things, too. Things in the sea, their eyes raised just above the water. They were watching her, blinking slowly, flicking their tentacles like cats' tails.

"Told you she'd wake up," said Scree.

Sophie touched the side of her head, which was damp with blood. She imagined her skull cracked open like an egg, the yolk of her brain spilling out, but she squeezed her eyes shut and told herself not to be so stupid. All the same, the air felt thick and heavy, and she couldn't breathe too well. It felt like there was a stone pressing on her lungs.

"I fell down," she said stupidly.

"All faculties intact, apparently," said Cartwright from somewhere to her left. "Including her amazing ability to state the obvious."

Feeling sick, Sophie rolled over and dislodged an octopus sitting on her chest. It looked at her mournfully until she scrabbled around in the wreckage by her head and found a damp biscuit, which she threw into the sea, much to its delight.

"You could have moved it," she said to Cartwright, who had cuts all over his face. She couldn't bring herself to feel annoyed. All she felt was a deep, almost painful relief, now that the world was quiet again. Manic stood behind him, chewing lumps of brick.

"It refused," he said. "It just sat there making squelching noises and spraying ink. It's all over you, by the way."

She looked at her blood-covered hand again, which wasn't covered in blood but the strange misery of the octopus. She climbed to her feet, wincing at the pain in her shoulder, and turned to view the island. It was flat, and gray, and faded into the sea like someone had stamped on it and pushed it into the water. Everything had a burned-out look, and she felt a deep, unexpected pang of sorrow.

"We're not going to cure the Sea Fever, are we?" she asked, feeling empty.

"It was a stupid idea," said Cartwright. "There's no magic vial of medicine."

"That's 'cause there's no such thing as Sea Fever," said Scree.

Sophie and Cartwright stared at him.

"That's not true," said Sophie as a toe-tentacled squid flopped over her ankles, squelching. Her head was beginning to clear. "*Something* drove everyone mad."

"It wasn't a disease," countered Scree.

"I don't understand," said Cartwright.

"It's just people being scared," said Scree. "Mebbe someone got eaten by a sea creature one day, or a man drowned, but nobody put it down to bad luck. It got bigger till we didn't trust the water, or anything in it. The fear got out of control, and everyone thought it was a fever.

"It's called mass hysteria," added Scree. "Before the sea, it was fear of machines. Before machines, it was fear of the dark. 'Course, most times nobody made up a magical island for everyone to go to."

Cartwright briefly looked like he wanted to jump into the sea.

"Mister Scree," Sophie said, "what are we supposed to do now?"

"What happens," he said, "is you get out of this place. You go to the mainland and get that shoulder seen to, then you go into the world and do whatever young people do."

"What about you?" she said. "I'm not running off and leaving you alone!"

"I'm staying here, girl, in the catacombs and caves. I'm too old to leave them, and this rock is in my blood. I'll eat glowfish and silverbugs and make a house from the rubble."

"It'll be lonely," said Sophie.

"But we're used to that here, aren't we?" he said, his crooked smile cracking his usually sour face. "I'm not going anywhere. I'd disintegrate and blow about like dust if I left."

"If the creatures get hungry—"

"You seen them?" he said, pointing at the water. "They're not staying here. They'll go wherever you go. They're yours now."

And there they were, hundreds of them, lined up in the water like an audience, watching her without moving, their heads poking up out of the waves. She got up and walked slowly to the fringe of the beach, and when she entered the water they still didn't do a thing. Not one creature opened its mouth.

She looked at Scree nervously.

"You understand them," he said. "And you're not scared. They like that."

"Shoes," she said to her uncomprehending audience.

They stared at her with their thousands of eyes. "When I came here, I lost my shoes in the water. I need some more. Come on, there must be tons of stuff floating around down there . . ."

Still nothing.

"Shoes," she repeated, and lifted a foot out of the water, wriggling her toes.

"She's gone nuts," Cartwright said behind her. Out in the sea, a barnacle-covered head sank like a periscope, and a minute later reemerged in front of her, pushing a mass of creatures out of its way. Sophie stepped back as it belched. A pair of leather shoes landed at her feet. The laces were knotted together in a slimy mess, the soles peeling away, holes in the toes, bloated and gray—but they were hers. They had to be. Her old boots had been rescued from the sea.

"They like me," she said, shocked, turning to Scree and Cartwright. "I think they're beginning to understand me."

"Aye," said Scree. "They're head over heels with you. Use 'em wisely."

"I will," she said.

He gave her a crafty look. His knees creaked as he sat down on a lump of fallen building. "I reckon you ought to tell a story on an occasion like this."

338

Sophie, touched, sat down, too, with the boots in her hand. She tried to think of a way to start. Then she looked into the wreckage of the building and began.

***

The Caretaker's Ghost
In Which We Find That an End Is a Beginning

Once there was an island, and the island was at the end of its life.

It was surrounded by a trembling black sea and a freezing sky. There was nothing left on it but weeds and bones and a few luminescent glowfish trapped in its underground tunnels. The sea creatures that used to live there were hibernating deep under the waves. It was as quiet and lonely as the inside of a clam.

Deep down in the heart of the island there was a ghost, the island's caretaker. He had been a man, and a glowfish, and a drop of water, and now he was in the very fabric of the rock. He had slept for hundreds of years, dreaming of the house he used to look after and the wonderful stories he used to tell. Only now, at the end of all things, was he waking up.

He didn't recognize the place in front of him. The grand old house had crumbled. The trees were bent over with cold, and the ground was choked with shaggy moss and cruel-looking weeds. Everything was gray and miserable.

The ghost rose from the catacombs. He had an idea. He would start again.

He called to the glowfish that lurked sadly in the depths of the tunnels and showed them the way into the sea. They jumped to life and swam rapidly away. The caretaker turned over every stone and chased away the shadows living beneath them. He pulled the thorny weeds out of the ground, then coaxed the trees back to life. He found a beautiful red stone abandoned by the shore, and after polishing it, he tossed it into the water as a gift for the queen of the sea.

That night, the queen received her gift. She picked the red stone up, and its warmth melted the ice at the tips of her fingers. As she held it, the frost around her heart began to drip away as well.

While the caretaker was sleeping, the queen traveled to the island and started to rebuild the house. When she finished she roused the sea monsters, so that the caretaker would never be lonely.

The caretaker woke to find the island exactly as it had been years before, with the beautiful house standing tall and the monsters playing in the sea. The garden was thick with greenery, and for the first time in years snow-white gulls circled overhead. Smiling, the caretaker resurrected an old deck chair. He opened it, sat down, put his hands behind his head, and yawned.

Years later, on the shore of the island, oysters began to grow.

***

Sophie and Cartwright were on the beach facing the mainland, hanging from Manic, who was chomping his jaws at the sea with horrible enthusiasm. Scree stood behind them on a pile of stone, his hand raised in a salute.

"I still don't know how we're going to get across," murmured Cartwright in Sophie's ear. "I mean, I feel bad for stamping on them now. It's almost like they have personalities."

"Just do it," she said. "I think everything will work itself out."

They cantered toward the sea, and Manic, happy to be free again, started to gallop. Sophie clung to the reins for dear life as they hurtled toward the gray ocean and the clouds curdling on the horizon. They were about to ride into a tempest.

They hit the water, but before Manic could go any farther a crab the size of a flattened bed heaved itself from the bottom of the sea and brought them flying up to the surface. Things lined up in front of them, jellyfish and more crabs and a small flat whale, and Manic hurtled from one to the other, bewildered by their cooperation.

The wind hit them in their faces, making their lips turn blue and their cheeks sting. But Sophie had never felt more at home.

"I know what I'm going to do," she yelled over the sound of the churning sea. The dark sky gathered above them like a pool of ink as they flew over the surf. "I'm going to travel, and I'll take my monsters to the ends of the earth with me. I *can* cure Sea Fever. I can show anyone who listens that the creatures are just animals, and the sea is their home. I'll show everybody that the water is just another place, and write everything down, and tell the stories over and over so nobody forgets. Maybe I'll even find a real new continent. There must be one out there, somewhere, in all that water." She gave Cartwright a sidelong glance. "You can come with me, if you want."

"You wouldn't last a minute without me anyway," he scoffed, then yelped as something nipped his foot.

"If you get annoying, they have my full permission to eat you."

And then something huge and black reared from the waves, reaching out to them with a forest of arms and pulling them down into the sea.

A moment of ice and utter darkness. A terrifying pang of doubt. Then they broke the surface again, twined in the thick, blubbery arms of a monster, which held them aloft as they sailed into the heart of the storm.

Acknowledgments

My endless thanks go to all the people who helped turn *The Bone Snatcher* from a crazy story swimming around my head to a Real Life Book that you can hold, smell, and prop the door open with (unless you have the electronic version—but still).

First of all, to my agent, Kirsty McLachlan, who saw tentacles waving through a sea of manuscripts and decided to give Sophie a go—and has pretty much organized every aspect of my writing life since. Also to the great team at Rights People, including Allison Hellegers, for all their help in placing the book.

Secondly, to the team at Dial Books for Young Readers; particularly to Stacey Friedberg, a wonderful editor who tirelessly worked to make the story everything it is today, and who made the whole (sometimes terrifying) thing a lot easier.

I am also grateful to the Comyn People—namely Eric Baron, Richard O'Halloran, and Tom Stewart—for reading the first few chapters over and over, and giving me more great ideas, and cups of tea, than I could have managed alone.

Thanks also to Emil Rybczak, for generally keeping me alive while I write, and for not playing the piano as loudly as he could.

And last, but certainly not least, to all the friends, family, and teachers who have encouraged me to keep going, given me invaluable help and advice, and invested their time and effort in guiding me. You know who you are, and you're all my heroes.

Charlotte Salter lives in England, and has a Master's in Writing. *The Bone Snatcher* is her debut book. Like her protagonist, Charlotte loves to tell stories and create dark, fantastical worlds. Learn more at https://charlotte-salter.com or follow Charlotte online @CeSalter.

31901060309400